NEW BEGINNINGS

Also by Alma Kennedy Bowen

The Cement Duck

NEW BEGINNINGS

ALMA KENNEDY BOWEN

New Beginnings

Copyright © 2020 by Alma Kennedy Bowen. All rights reserved.

No part of this publication may be reproduced, stored in a retrieval system or transmitted in any way by any means, electronic, mechanical, photocopy, recording or otherwise without the prior permission of the author except as provided by USA copyright law.

The opinions expressed by the author are not necessarily those of URLink Print and Media.

1603 Capitol Ave., Suite 310 Cheyenne, Wyoming USA 82001
1-888-980-6523 | admin@urlinkpublishing.com

URLink Print and Media is committed to excellence in the publishing industry.

Book design copyright © 2020 by URLink Print and Media. All rights reserved.

Published in the United States of America
ISBN 978-1-64753-393-9 (Paperback)
ISBN 978-1-64753-394-6 (Hardback)
ISBN 978-1-64753-395-3 (Digital)

02.06.20

For
Heather, Breanna, Erika, and Emily

CONTENTS

BENNIE

Chapter 1: Spring Cove 11
Chapter 2: Cousin Melvin 17
Chapter 3: Overhill Road 21
Chapter 4: The Hotel 30
Chapter 5: The Sawmill 35
Chapter 6: The Restaurant 42
Chapter 7: Churched 47
Chapter 8: Traveling Preacher 51
Chapter 9: The Stranger 56
Chapter 10: Atlanta Tourists 62
Chapter 11: Fannie Mae 68
Chapter 12: He Returns 72
Chapter 13: The Father 77
Chapter 14: Not Another Daddy 82
Chapter 15: Hank Loves Me 86
Chapter 16: The Killer 91
Chapter 17: Cousin Dorothy 95
Chapter 18: The Buggy Ride 100
Chapter 19: The Renter 106
Chapter 20: Christmas 110
Chapter 21: A Damaged Soul 115
Chapter 22: The Train 120
Chapter 23: Ellie 124
Chapter 24: Caleb 129

KATHERINE

Chapter 1: 1932 137
Chapter 2: A Job 141
Chapter 3: Umbrella 148
Chapter 4: Her Eyes 154
Chapter 5: Stop At Bob's 157
Chapter 6: Cyclorama 162
Chapter 7: No One To Mourn 166
Chapter 8: Mountains' Trees 169
Chapter 9: Dark Side 174
Chapter 10: The Registrars 178
Chapter 11: Voting Day 184
Chapter 12: Mr. Woody 188
Chapter 13: Picture Quilt 192
Chapter 14: To Washington 195
Chapter 15: Tree Army 201
Chapter 16: Home Again 208

BENNIE

CHAPTER 1

SPRING COVE

How can I write to him? What words will I use? Bennie was almost overwhelmed with questions. How could she write letters to the preacher? What would she call him in her letters? She had never before spoken his actual name.

She grabbed her two girls and went straight home after he suggested they should exchange letters. He was leaving, and she didn't want to talk to people at the church. She wanted to be alone to think about what she had promised. Sitting on the front porch of her cousin's house, the only home she had in Helen, Bennie began to think about her life. When she was fourteen years old—it seemed so long ago—another preacher had broke her heart. He'd told her she could no longer attend his church. She had deeply missed her friends in Sunday school and vowed to never set foot in another church. After many refusals, she finally attended this preacher's services, and now he said he wanted her to be his wife. He was different, but if she married him, he might not be able to continue preaching. People would not like a preacher whose wife had been *churched*, meaning she could no longer attend church.

Back when she decided to come to Helen, back when she considered the town bizarre and dangerous, she promised herself she would go back home after Katherine had been in school three years. Now the three years would be over in a few months when Katherine finished the third grade, but she couldn't go back to Tray Mountain.

She had enough money. She had learned all she needed to know about town people and the strange new conveniences of the twentieth century. But she now had another little girl who would need to begin school. She had not expected to accumulate new obligations after she arrived in 1913. If she left now, no one would take care of her cousin's house. Little Angel would not be able to attend school.

Bennie had not expected to become indebted in any way in Helen, but she was deeply beholden. Incredible new changes in her life now emblazoned her mind with memories.

Before she died, her mother had told Bennie she must go where no one knew about her and her daughter. She had to find a new place to live, but she never once dreamed about going to the new sawmill town of Helen. She and her friend, Ellie Rigsby, shared many opinions about the new town. The two women lived about four miles apart on Tray Mountain and had no other neighbors.

They knew about Helen because every word about the sawmill traveled across the northern Georgia mountains faster than a summer storm. There was no newspaper or radio station to announce the massive new business venture, but men left their homes with excitement, hurrying to take part in the amazing new lifestyle.

The Helen sawmill was the largest sawmill east of the Mississippi River, and its sharp, thin saw blades could slice giant logs in an instant. The town's newfangled electricity made the saws daringly fast, and throughout their lives, Ellie and Bennie had heard horror stories about the much slower man-operated saws and axes where men lost fingers and hands. These new saws at Helen could kill a man or, worse, injure him so badly he'd wish he had been killed. No person with good sense would want to work around such danger, the two women agreed.

People in the sawmill's surrounding village bragged about their electric lights and flush toilets. No person needed such things. Bennie and Ellie were proud of their oil lanterns, mule power, and outhouses.

NEW BEGINNINGS

And they heard that Helen's passenger/freight train made such loud noises it frightened farm animals. Neither woman could compare stories about the Helen train to anything else in their lives and couldn't imagine how it worked or how fast it traveled.

Despite being aware of the bizarre differences, Bennie Sheldon decided early in August to leave her home on Tray Mountain and move to the new town. She reminded herself more than once that she shouldn't be afraid, because her mother always told her that a special angel watched over her.

She sat on her front porch one morning, waiting to tell the peddler her decision. Her daughter, Katherine, sat beside her, and Duke, the family's old hound, sat at their feet. They talked about the blue sky and the mockingbird singing in the tall trees above them before both became silent, and Bennie thought about her mother, who had died four months earlier. Bennie's mother had whispered words through fever to tell her that she must leave their beloved home in Tray Mountain's Spring Cove.

Bennie thought Spring Cove belonged to her personally. "We must celebrate the beauty of the mountains and Spring Cove," her mother had said many times. Now Bennie was responsible for Spring Cove because she had no brothers or sisters. She was a complete surprise to her parents, who'd thought they couldn't have children.

Her father's death four years earlier was easier to accept than her mother's because he had been sick for years and rarely spoke. But her mother's quick death left a gaping hole in Bennie's life.

For four days, Marie Sheldon had drifted in and out of a coma. On the fifth day, Ellie Rigsby's oldest son went to Helen for the doctor. Soon after he arrived, the doctor talked to Marie Sheldon about death, and after he left, Marie began slowly talking about life—Bennie's life.

Bennie tried to keep her mother quiet as she put water on her fevered lips and bathed her face with a cool cloth, but every word cut deep into her mind. "You must find another home here in the mountains, a place where no one knows you. And you need to learn about people."

The second day after the doctor's visit, Marie began to look young and relaxed. Bennie was bathing her face once again with a cool cloth when she realized that Marie's forehead was as cold as a creek rock. She dropped her head to her chest, didn't hear a heartbeat, and picked up her mother's hand. It was limp.

She was dead.

As Bennie slowly understood the situation, her mind fell into a bottomless pit. She became desperately lonely and vulnerable. Marie Sheldon had been her living sanctuary, her place of complete safety. She never doubted Marie's love for her, and Marie loved Katherine before her granddaughter was born, before Bennie learned to love her.

Slowly Bennie realized that she must clean and dress her mother. She delicately pulled the worn nightgown and drawers off her mother's fragile figure. She carefully bathed her and then dressed her in a white embroidered cotton dress made from treasured flour sacks. She put a matching cap with handmade lace on her head, tied a big bow under her chin, and kissed her cold forehead.

Sunlight was completely gone, and Katherine was asleep in bed. Bennie still wanted to notify Ellie and her family. She would give the "I need you" signal used by all families in this era because telephones still were not available. She picked up the shotgun, walked outside the door, and cut the silence by firing three quick shots into the night sky. *Bam! Bam! Bam!*

Four miles away, the mother, father, and six sons at the Rigsbys' heard the signal. The two oldest sons hurried through the night to Bennie's side, where they then talked about burial.

Now her mother had been gone four months, and sometimes Bennie still sat straight up in her bed at night because she thought Marie had called her.

Bennie was waiting to tell the peddler her decision to go to Helen because she wanted to tell someone before she changed her mind again. Bennie didn't want to tell Ellie that she must go to a place where people didn't know her background, because Ellie knew everything about her.

Was that the creaking sound of Mr. Williams's wagon wheels? Maybe it was a breeze in the trees again because Duke hadn't raised his head.

"Can you hear him, Kat?"

Katherine, who had fallen asleep, didn't answer.

She planned to accept her cousin's offer to provide a room for her, but she didn't actually know him. Her cousin liked his life in Helen, where all kinds of people lived so close together they couldn't cuss a cat without getting fur in their teeth. *I'll have to get dressed just to go to the outhouse.* She had seen him only once, and he had never seen her daughter.

Suddenly Duke raised his head, leaped up, and ran toward the road. Slowly the peddler pulled up, and Bennie didn't give him time to ask once again about her life in Spring Cove with only a child for companionship.

"Mr. Williams, I've made a decision. Please tell Cousin Melvin that I hope he can find a job for me."

"Helen ain't got jobs fer women," Williams said. He came from generations of mountaineers. As a young child, Bennie had tried to speak exactly like him and been severely corrected by her mother, who'd once planned to be a schoolteacher.

Bennie stared at him without responding. *You can't change my mind. I have to have a job.*

Williams spread news as he peddled household items, and on each monthly visit for at least the past three years, he had talked excitedly about the new sawmill and the new town named Helen. After Bennie only stared at him, Williams agreed to pass her decision to Melvin Rhodes. "I have to get Kat in school," Bennie said. That required courage. *I must have a backup plan if the schoolteacher won't accept Kat.*

"They got a real school buildin' now and ain't using that ol' train car anymore. Learnin's free to the Helen chil'ren, an' it's open each year longer than schools fer farm kids. You can move and get settled in by the time it's open ag'in. But where'll you live?"

"Cousin Melvin said he and his wife have an extra room."

Williams said everyone he knew was working for the sawmill. He talked about the Rigsbys' son who got a job working at the woods hicks' camp on Wildcat Creek. "It's a good thing that Miz Rigsby's married and a couple o' her chil'ren are 'bout grown. She ain't a young woman livin' alone like you. Yore still a young'un, ain't you?"

"I'm nineteen," Bennie said defensively and changed the subject. "How much are you giving for sang?"

She used the common slang term for the exotic ginseng plant found in the Georgia mountains and exported to China, where it was considered a love stimulant. Months earlier, she'd been relieved to find mature plants in the distant woods. She harvested four roots, each shaped like a tiny human pelvis with two fleshy legs, and dried them in the sun.

"I kin give jest a doller ah ounce. Ya know how that price jumps up 'n' down." He took out a metal scale, and Bennie handed him the dried ginseng roots wrapped in a white cloth. He put them on the scale and said, "This ain't quite four ounces, but they's really fine. I say it's a full four dollars."

"The only thing I can buy today is a thimble," she said. "I left my mother's old thimble here on the steps one day, and it disappeared."

She selected a thimble that fit her middle finger and gave him three pennies. Williams counted out three paper one-dollar bills with two silver half-dollar coins and gave them to Bennie for the ginseng. "I'm glad yer goin' ta Helen. It's sure 'nuf a fancy place, and yer gonna be 'roun' a lotta people, mos' of 'em good, but some notsa good," he said.

CHAPTER 2

COUSIN MELVIN

Nine days later, Duke barked the announcement of a visitor. Bennie's heart beat faster as the early morning sunlight fell on a sleek horse and beautiful traveling apparatus.

If that's Cousin Melvin, I can't back out now.

The driver jumped down, took off his black derby hat, and bowed toward her, saying, "You must be Cousin Bennie. You've grown up."

Bennie quickly lowered her eyes. Cousin Melvin appeared extremely large at more than six feet tall, compared to Bennie's barefooted five feet and five inches. One-inch heels on his boots made him appear even taller as did his full-length, light gray travel duster.

Melvin had left Helen before daylight, so Bennie shyly invited him to sit on the porch while she quickly stirred hot coals in the cookstove, fried an egg for him, and put it in one of that morning's leftover biscuits.

The son of her mother's deceased sister, Cousin Melvin was the only living relative Bennie knew. The nation's first gold rush was nearing its final public throes when he arrived in Auraria, a town about thirty-five miles west of Helen. A few years after he visited them, he wrote that he was married and working in the new sawmill office. His letter praised the lumber business, plans for the train, and the mill's enormous size.

After the death of Bennie's mother, the peddler brought a letter from Melvin asking Bennie to bring Katherine and live with him and his wife. Bennie had not met his wife and was surprised at the invitation.

Melvin bowed toward her again. "We're glad you're coming to Helen. You can live with us, and you won't have to get a job."

After Bennie didn't answer, he said, "A real lady doesn't work outside the home. It's not respectable. A fellow wants a wife who can make him comfortable at home, a woman who is not part of a man's rough world."

Bennie had plowed their garden each spring, shot a deer each year to make dried venison, and, with her mother three years earlier, had slaughtered their last hog with meat to be salt-cured, canned or given away. As a mountain woman, success with "man's work" was necessary, although sewing was her favorite task.

Melvin talked enthusiastically about the town but said nothing to change Bennie's mind about working. He said the Helen doctor and nurse were available full-time at the company's medical clinic. The mill was growing so fast that the company had to build two hotels for laborers. The Commercial Hotel on Main Street was complete, and The Marshall, on the mountain overlooking the mill, was almost finished.

The Mountain Ranch Hotel, not owned by the sawmill company, was also on Main Street and was being used as a clubhouse by the mill managers.

He finally admitted that the manager of the new Mountain Ranch Hotel said Bennie might have a job there. "He didn't make a promise," Melvin said.

While she was packing, Cousin Melvin drove to the Rigsbys' house to explain her departure. One of the Rigsbys' sons was coming that evening to catch the Sheldons' chickens once they were roosting.

Bennie deeply regretted that she hadn't told Ellie goodbye. Mr. Horace Rigsby was never present when Bennie visited, and Ellie never mentioned him. After Bennie began to wonder if Ellie's husband was dead, she saw him staggering around the barn. Marie said he probably had a drinking problem.

Ellie Rigsby could never leave her home because her severely handicapped son, Wayne, fifteen years old, was bedridden and unable to walk or talk. Bennie had been present more than once when Mrs. Rigsby removed a dirty diaper from her son. His skinny, hairy legs made her aware that his mother had been feeding him, cleaning him, and washing his dirty diapers for fifteen years. *Maybe he cannot speak with his mouth, but he speaks with his eyes*, Bennie thought, because Wayne's eyes followed his mother around the room.

Mrs. Rigsby had always wanted a baby girl but had only boys. Just two months earlier, she gave birth to a baby girl who weighed two pounds. The baby was kept in a shoebox on the warm floor behind the cookstove when she wasn't nursing at her mother's breast, and Bennie was amazed that she was growing. Soon the family would have to choose a name for her.

Bennie only had to think about Ellie Rigsby's never-ending tasks to know that her own life was good.

Now their clothes were packed, and they were dressed for travel. Bennie and Katherine wore faded long-sleeved dresses, wide-brimmed bonnets, and cotton gloves. Their attire had been carefully sewn to never let sunlight directly touch their skin. She knew that pale skin was a badge of wisdom and success, while yokels and hicks had multiple freckles and tanned skin.

Bennie's mother was surprised that her little girl had auburn hair. When Bennie was older, her mother told her not to complain because her hair caused extra effort to protect her skin. "You have sun-kissed hair. You don't need sun on your face and arms," she said. "All the angels have sun hair like yours."

Bennie's and Kat's belongings were packed in the luggage trunk that her mother used back in 1867 to travel to northern Georgia with her father. After Cousin Melvin put the trunk in his buggy, Bennie put Kat on the seat, tied a rope around Duke's neck, and fastened him to the back of the buggy.

Climbing into the seat, she looked back at her home. Another person would see only an old log structure, but the cabin was Bennie's heart home. In her mind, she saw images of her daddy building a fire in the fireplace or cookstove, and her mother straining milk, canning vegetable soup, laughing at some unexpected comment, or rocking baby Katherine.

Melvin picked up the reins and clucked, and the horse moved forward. "Helen is taking advantage of the new wonders of the twentieth century. After all, this is 1913. We have to help each other. You'll probably find a husband in Helen because we have a lot of single men. Let me warn you now, we have a few Yankees, and they're stingy and mean. You can't trust a Yankee," he said.

Bennie's mother had warned her about Yankees many times and described how Bennie's grandfather had fought in the Confederacy and lost his valuable horse while he was in a Yankee prison. She stiffened her shoulders and looked straight ahead without saying a word. *I will not be friends with any person, certainly not a man.*

CHAPTER 3

OVERHILL ROAD

Cousin Melvin's buggy turned onto the shady mountain road easily rolling six miles west, passing the church Bennie attended before Katherine was born. In her mind's eye, she saw the scripture verses painted on the walls and the graves of her mother and daddy, each marked with a large stone. She wondered if the church still held all-day singings and dinner on the grounds.

The buggy turned south onto the much wider red-dirt road, Unicoi Turnpike. The sky was blue without a single cloud, and the road was filled with August sun. Bennie pulled her bonnet forward to be sure her face was totally shaded, tugged on her sleeves and gloves, and looked at Kat to make sure her face and hands were protected while their dresses covered their bare feet.

"I'm glad the weather's been dry. Wheels get hub-deep in red mud on this road after it rains awhile," Melvin said. As he spoke, he guided the horse to the right side of the road to avoid deep ruts on the left.

Melvin talked about Helen and its sawmill the way an enamored man might talk about a beautiful woman. He rejoiced in the country's industrial revolution, which provided exciting new opportunities for men. The steam power, electricity, and machines that replaced hand production had finally reached the Georgia mountains.

Bennie found it hard to respond to his comments. She was thinking about her father who had called the turnpike Overhill

Road. Her father had taken her by horseback along the road and back trails to the new Nacoochee Institute, the Presbyterian boarding school that had opened in Sautee Valley. She was nine years old, and her mother already had taught her. Bennie could read and write, and she had memorized the multiplication tables. After she took a test at the school, she was placed in the fourth grade where she discovered history and geography. She began dreaming of seeing the world and writing about her adventures.

She was able to stay at the school only four months. A teacher's son took her back home on horseback because her father had become gravely ill. He lived six more years, but Bennie didn't return to school, and she always regretted it.

"Like I said, I don't know much about the hotel, but it's really nice. The only time I've been in it is when I went to talk to Herman Knox about giving you a job," Melvin said.

The buggy's iron wheels lurched again over one of the many rocks, and Bennie grabbed the seat with one hand and Kat with the other. "I hope Mr. Knox will let me work there," she said.

"The two trains are operating now. The logging train is a new Shay locomotive, strong enough to climb these mountains as it goes to the timber camps. The other is a passenger/freight that travels to Gainesville. That town is more than thirty miles south of Helen, but if you ride the train, you can go to Gainesville, visit the stores, and come back all in the same day."

"I wouldn't want to go that fast."

"Oh, you will enjoy the train. It provides amazing travel, and the rail tracks were not easy to put in place. You should see some of the giant trestles they built across the valleys between the mill and the timber camps. One is sixty feet high and a hundred feet long." Melvin drew a deep breath before he added, "The mill is almost unbelievable. It's going to take timber from fifty- six square miles in the counties of White, Towns, Union, and Habersham.

"Woods hicks come here from sawmills in other states, and they say they've never seen a mill this big before. Seventeen acres are cut each day with all the logs brought to the mill just to keep the band saw going."

Bennie knew that men who worked at sawmills were called woods hicks, but she had no concept of the band saw. "How is a band saw different?" she said.

"The band saw is twice as fast as a circular saw, and its kerf is smaller. That means it makes a very thin cut through the wood." Melvin was explaining, but he was talking about electric saws, and Bennie had not even seen an electric lightbulb.

She felt she had to rise above her ignorance and anxiety and say something to Melvin. "I wonder how much they paid for so much land."

"The bank where the owners applied for a loan appraised the land at about thirty-nine dollars an acre, but I'm sure they didn't pay anywhere near that amount. A woods hick who came here from Arkansas said good timberland out there was sometimes going for a dollar-twenty-five an acre. Some even sold for fifty cents an acre," Melvin said, shaking his head in disbelief. He slowed the horse and swerved to the right side of the road as they met a large, heavily loaded wagon pulled by four oxen. Its slow progress raised little dust. Melvin tipped his hat toward the driver and said, "They're probably going to Towns County. I heard that the Methodist College there has built a new dormitory."

The only thing Bennie knew about Towns County was that it was on the far side of the mountains next to Union County, and both counties had opposed the South's withdrawal from the nation before the War between the States.

"Our neighbor's son is working for the sawmill. I guess he's glad to be a woods hick," she said.

"They start out making fifty cents a day, and if they stay with it, they can eventually get a dollar a day," Melvin said, adding that some people didn't like the sawmill.

Mountain families had no need for money. Generations earlier, lucky white men won their land in one of Georgia's land lotteries, which distributed acreage formerly owned by the Cherokee Indian

Nation. The 1829 gold rush caused the government to make the northeast Georgia land available after forcibly removing the Indians.

Like Bennie's fiercely independent parents, the lottery winners and their descendants had built their own cabins; harvested their own vegetables, fruits, and meats; woven their own cloth; and made their own clothes. Business deals were trade transactions, such as a dozen new locust fence posts to a blacksmith for a new iron plow blade.

When a husband began daily work at the mill, the plowing, livestock care, roof repair, and fence repair—all the chores he had previously done—became responsibilities of his wife and children. For some families, this change caused major discontent.

Melvin began talking about the timber camps that were set up beside the new mountain railway spurs. A camp included temporary housing for families of the woods hicks and company kitchens with chow halls. "Some of the houses have two or three rooms, and the rooms are separated and hauled to new locations on the train. The heater and any large furniture pieces are fastened to the walls, and if it's going to a new family, each room is steam- cleaned before it's moved."

"Sometimes we can see the steam clouds from the mill. At first, we thought it was a lot of smoke, but Mr. Williams told us what it was," Bennie said.

"The steam you saw from your home is from tall pipes that you'll see when we get to Helen. There're five of them. Steam turns generators to make electricity. We have hoppers underneath the saws that catch all the sawdust, and it's blown into the boiler that feeds the steam engines. Wood scraps feed the boiler too. The mill is an extremely clean operation. The owners have even put large incinerators in each of the railroad camps to burn all the waste. They're doing everything possible to avoid sickness."

Bennie didn't know how to respond to most of his comments, but she listened carefully. She expected him to ask her about Kat's father before they got to Helen, and she had an answer prepared. But he talked on and on without asking her anything about herself.

NEW BEGINNINGS

The sun had passed the overhead mark and moved to the western sky when Bennie took biscuits from a cotton bag. She handed one to Kat and another to Cousin Melvin, keeping one for herself. As they ate, all three became thirsty.

They rode into the small community called Robertstown. Cousin Melvin stopped the buggy before they reached a large building called Roberts Store. He and Bennie jumped down, and Bennie helped Katherine down so they could go sip water from the Chattahoochee River. Barns and large gardens were beside or behind each of the nearby houses. Bennie was relieved to see that the homes had enough space for patches of tall corn, beans, and other fresh vegetables.

After passing Roberts Store, Cousin Melvin halted the buggy to give a coin to the gatekeeper. The long pike or pole that crossed the road turned to let the buggy pass. "Now I guess you know why this road is called a turnpike," Melvin said.

The road followed the Chattahoochee River, first on one side and then the other. They forded the shallow river twice, and it was rushing and splashing beside the road when the buggy slowed down behind four covered wagons. Children and women walked beside the wagons, and most of them returned Melvin's nod with a wave. Bennie and Katherine waved back.

"They're coming back from a camping trip," Melvin said. "That's a popular pastime for Helen families on the weekends." He did not explain that the families left their homes on weekends because that was when the woods hicks came in from the lumber camps and drank too much corn whiskey, becoming loud, disruptive, and obnoxious.

The sun was almost gone when Cousin Melvin pulled off the turnpike, which had become Helen's Main Street. Bennie saw rows of new framed and painted buildings—some red, some gray—on both sides of the road, and she didn't see a single building made of logs. She could see yards that were swept clean and people sitting on porches while their laughing, hollering children played in the road.

"There's the apothecary, and we have a bank, boarding house, barbershop, and café. The railroad operates a commissary just across the river, and it has excellent meats and foodstuffs," Melvin said.

Bennie didn't speak but knew she could buy remedies for different ailments at the apothecary and was relieved to know Helen had places to buy food.

The pleasant scent of freshly sawed lumber filled the air, and Bennie saw the five tall pipes reaching into the sky. "I thought you said steam came from those pipes," she said.

"This is Sunday. The sawmill doesn't operate on Sundays," Melvin said.

He guided the buggy to the back of a house that was larger than the others, and a tall woman with light brown hair came out to welcome them. "I'm glad you're here," she said. Melvin introduced her as his wife, Dorothy.

"Come with me and see your room," she said.

Bennie grabbed Kat's hand, and they went up three wooden steps before opening a screen door into a small room. "You see, you have your own entrance so you can be as private as you wish," Cousin Dorothy said. "This room was added to our house for storage, but it has a window. It's small, but I hope you and your little girl will feel at home here."

The room had an ornate iron bed painted a golden-bronze color. A strange tufted white coverlet designed in beautiful flower images of yellow, green, blue, and red lay across the bed, and there were two pillows.

Cousin Dorothy pointed to a chamber pot and said, "You can use that in the middle of the night, and we have a flush toilet. You can empty the chamber in our toilet. It's next to our bedroom."

Bennie didn't say anything. She knew human body waste collected in a large hole underneath a toilet. *If they have a toilet inside the house, the odor is going to be unbearable.*

One lightbulb with a short string hung down from the ceiling over the bed. Pointing at the bulb, Dorothy said, "Helen has electric lights, and they flash each night at five minutes till ten before they go off at ten o'clock. They come back on at five each morning." She reached up, pulled the string, and the bulb became bright.

"This room is good, but we can't keep this coverlet," Bennie said.

Dorothy looked puzzled, and said, "This is called a chenille spread, and it was made by a woman in Dalton over in West Georgia. Her coverlets are becoming famous everywhere, and I found this one in Gainesville." She smiled. "I think the word *chenille* is perfect because it's the French word for hairy caterpillar."

Bennie said, "The bed will be our only place to sit down, and I don't want to come in from work and sit on such a beautiful cover. We can use one of our quilts, and we have our own pillows and sheets."

"We want you to be comfortable here," Dorothy said, handing her a skeleton key. "This is the key to your outside door."

Still holding Kat's hand, Bennie followed Dorothy into the kitchen.

She couldn't stop staring at every item. It was not like anything she had imagined. The cookstove was a shiny black, and the dishes looked delicate, not sturdy and strong like her dishes at home. They rested inside a glossy glass cabinet with a matching walnut sideboard and table. Dorothy talked about the fun she had shopping at a big furniture store in downtown Gainesville.

The parlor, with its store-bought blue upholstered settee and chairs, also left Bennie silent and staring while Dorothy said the covering was silk brocade with a Turkish design. Dorothy used the word *tête-à-tête* instead of *settee* and pointed to a large plush chair, saying it was Melvin's chair. Bennie stared at the thick, silky fringe around the bottom of all three pieces. Lamps beside each chair also were very strange to her.

Wondering where her cousin got money for such an elaborate home, she said, "Are all the Helen homes like this?"

"I haven't been inside many other homes, but I can tell you this. I'm proud to be your cousin's wife, proud of the home he built for us, and we're both glad to have you join us," Dorothy said. Suddenly, she added, "You can use my iron and ironing board too." She proceeded to show Bennie an electric iron and a padded board on folded wooden legs. Bennie picked up the iron and decided it was not heavy enough to iron nearly as well as the old, heated flatirons she had used at home.

Later, when they were eating fried ham, green beans, corn bread, and a slice of egg custard pie, Bennie learned that Dorothy had grown up in Atlanta and was visiting her grandparents in Dahlonega when she met Cousin Melvin. They had been married two years and wanted children. Dorothy told Bennie more than once to call on her if she could help with Katherine.

They invited Bennie and Kat to join them each Sunday in Bible study and worship services at one of the homes. Bennie thanked them for the invitation but did not tell them that she would never attend.

Later Bennie and Kat went outside to visit Duke where he was tied to the steps. Bennie gave him a large piece of Dorothy's corn bread and a piece of ham bone. Then she and Kat sat on the steps while they still could see lights in houses around them. Bennie knew she was right to leave her home in Spring Cove as her mother had said, but she didn't know that everything in Helen would be so strange. She thought about how a dragonfly hovered around and around over the creek, sometimes getting really close to the water. She was hovering here and there over a new life, but she wasn't going to get close. *I'm not a dragonfly. I'm the mockingbird, who stays high in the treetops.*

Kat wanted to know where the school was located, but Bennie didn't know. She could think only about going to see Mr. Knox the following morning.

After they lay down on top of the patchwork quilt, Katherine said, "Tell me again about this quilt." Like Bennie, Katherine wanted to step back into the familiar, and Marie Sheldon had used the quilt to talk about geography.

Enough light was coming through the window, so Bennie pointed to a red piece on the quilt. "This is South Carolina where your nana was a child, and this big green piece is the ocean. The ocean reaches from the United States, our country, to Great Britain, another country. Your nana went to school in a city called Charleston and studied until she could become a teacher. English was her favorite subject, and she loved to read. She always wanted you and me to speak good English. She taught school for only one year because she met your papa. They fell in love, married, and came here to Georgia." Bennie pointed to a blue patch next to the red piece. "This is Georgia where we live. This is Tennessee, and here's North Carolina and South Carolina. These other patches represent the other states. Arizona became a state last year, and now there are forty-eight states."

The familiar, soft, whirring sound of katydids floated through the window, the same sound that always put her to sleep back at the cabin. It was too dark in their room to see the quilt pieces, and Katherine was almost asleep. Bennie was overwhelmed with yearning for her mother and for home. She stopped talking to keep from bursting into tears.

CHAPTER 4

THE HOTEL

Before daylight the next morning, a loud piercing whistle caused Bennie to sit straight up in bed. Had a bear gone stark raving mad? Was Christ notifying the world He had returned? She heard no other sound. Had she imagined or dreamed that awful sound?

Bennie's heart was pounding when she remembered that she was in Helen at Melvin Rhodes's house. Katherine, lying close beside her, moaned, and it was the only sound. No one was screaming for help, so she would wait and see what happened. The room was pitch dark, and after gaining confidence, Bennie groped her way over to the window to look out. She saw lights come on in the next house, so the electricity apparently was available again.

She sat down on the bed trying to decide what to do when someone knocked softly on her inside door. "Who is it?" Bennie said.

Cousin Melvin's voice came through the door. "It's only five o'clock. I forgot to tell you about the work whistle. It's an old steamboat whistle from the Mississippi River, and it just blew at five o'clock to wake everyone. It'll give two short blasts at five minutes till seven, then a long blast at seven. At that time, everyone should have reported to work. You'll hear another blast at twelve noon and another at one o'clock. That's the time for workers to eat lunch. The blast at six o'clock tonight is quitting time."

"Thank you. What time should I see Mr. Knox?"

"I'd go see him at seven," Melvin said.

Bennie heard him walk away from the door, and she lay down again on the bed. She would have to wait two hours, and she didn't want to wake Kat. She listened to the sounds of Cousins Melvin and Dorothy in the other part of the house. Later she heard the soft voice of a neighbor calling goodbye.

She had a black skirt and a white waist, which some called a blouse, which she had made for her mother to wear to the church homecoming. Her mother didn't go, and the clothing had never been worn. The blouse with white embroidery was the color of newly fallen snow, and the skirt was black as midnight without stars. Both pieces were plain, and they projected class that her other clothing lacked.

After brushing and braiding her wavy, auburn hair, she twisted it on the back of her head. She heard two short whistle blasts as she put on the bonnet and cotton gloves.

She shook Kat and hugged her. "Please don't leave me, Mama," her daughter said with pleading eyes. "I have to go, but I won't be long. I'm going to see Mr. Knox. You are safe, and you must stay still and quiet," Bennie said. Katherine recalled the talks her mother had with her before they made the trip. She knew she must help her mother face difficult tasks, so she was quiet as Bennie stepped out and locked the door.

The sun still was behind the mountain, but the sky was light and the seven- o'clock whistle blew as she walked quickly across Main Street to the new Mountain Ranch Hotel. The train chugged by, going south, and blew its whistle. *Helen has a lot of loud noises.*

Although she did not pause for a better look as she walked up the hill toward the large porch, the green lawn and splashing water fountain with its lilies and goldfish were more beautiful than anything she had ever seen.

She stopped for a few seconds and stared when she saw big, strange, colorful birds slowly walking on the lawn here and there. The first sunrays popped across the mountaintop as one of the birds strutted beside the path with its delicate tail feathers spread up and out in a huge circle. The sun reflected off the jewel-like feathers in small, round, multicolored designs like eyes, here and there on the tail feathers. The birds probably were the peacocks Williams once told her about. "They're s'posed to show visitors that the Mountain Ranch Hotel is dif'rent and beautiful," he had said.

A nicely dressed man greeted her from the porch where a few men were sitting. She said, "I'm looking for Mr. Knox." He said he was Knox and invited her to follow him. They walked through a sitting room where a few more people were gathered and up the stairs to another large sitting room that was almost empty. He chose the seat farthest from a man and woman, the only two people there, and motioned for her to sit down. Bennie expected him to talk like sophisticated people she read about in a *Harper's Magazine*, but he talked like others in the mountains.

"What kin I do fer ya?" he said.

She removed her bonnet. "My name is Bennie Sheldon, and my cousin, Melvin Rhodes, said you might have a job for me." She thought of only one thing, getting a job so she could get Kat in school. She wasn't aware that her determination gave her face a striking radiance.

"Yore pore as a snake, but yore purty anuf."

Mr. Knox went on to say that the hotel still was being organized, and the only thing he could offer her was a job working in the kitchen and dining room. Bennie assured him that she could do that, and he said he would pay her twenty-five cents a day, six days a week.

"Ya gotta know a lot about this town 'cause ya can do a lot jest talkin' ta people. We want people to keep comin' here ag'in and ag'in."

Bennie kept nodding her head.

"When kin ya start?"

"I have a daughter, and I must find someone to look after her before I can begin," Bennie said.

"Tha's no problem. We have a half-breed widder woman here behin' the hotel who looks aidder kids. I kin show ya her house."

Bennie soon met Mrs. Ross, a half-Cherokee, who had two young children playing in her yard. Mrs. Ross said she didn't have children of her own but looked after a brother and sister whose mother had died. Their father, a woods hick, was staying at one of the camps. Bennie arranged to return with Kat for a visit.

She went back to the hotel and asked Mr. Knox what time she should be there to work the next morning. When he said "five o'clock," she was pleased. She had always enjoyed the morning's first sunlight.

Kat was dressed, sitting on the edge of the bed, and was delighted to see her mother when she got back to the room. She said Cousin Dorothy made fried egg biscuits for them and handed Bennie two biscuits, saying, "One of these is for Duke."

Dorothy knocked on the door and told Bennie she could empty her chamber pot. Although she silently objected, Bennie took the pot and followed Dorothy to their inside water toilet. She was expecting to see more strange things and didn't say anything as Dorothy showed her the handle to pull after she emptied her pot. Bennie did as instructed and was surprised when the toilet flushed into the town's sewerage system. She had never dreamed that any kind of toilet could be so clean and totally without odor.

Back with Katherine, she said, "Come with me. We're going to the store, and then I want you to visit a woman and two children who live behind the hotel."

"Why are we going to the store?" Kat said. "I want to go to the school."

Bennie explained that they would have to wait a few weeks before school began, and Kat's face lost its bright anticipation.

At the store, two heavily bearded old men were sitting on the porch, and inside, two women were talking about the value of an item. Bennie was pleased that no one spoke to her. She found a Blue Horse tablet and wooden No. 2 pencils to help Kat prepare for school. She found an alarm clock with a loud ring. She also bought herself a tablet with intentions to keep a daily journal, something she had wanted to do since she left school ten years ago.

After leaving the store, Bennie took Kat to Mrs. Ross's house. Mrs. Ross introduced her to the boy and girl—Hank, a third grader, and Goldie, a second grader. Goldie took one look at Kat and said the magic words "Let's play school." Kat was grinning excitedly when Bennie walked away.

Back in her room, Bennie changed into an old dress, sat on the steps to their room, and sharpened two of the pencils with the pocketknife that had once been her father's. She almost smiled as she remembered the man's comment as she paid him for the pencils: "Ya better sharpen these pencils yerself 'cause the teacher has a sharpenin' machine on her desk, 'n' the kids kin twist it and jest grind up ever' pencil."

Thinking she must do something to ease her worries, Bennie went back inside to redo the hurried stitches in her new apron. She sat on the bed and left the door open.

While sewing, she thought about her talk with Mr. Knox. Suddenly she remembered the man and woman sitting in the upstairs room. She had barely been aware of them, but now she realized that the woman was Ovaleen Birch, who had been her friend in church years before. Ovaleen didn't speak to her. *Maybe she didn't want anyone to know that she knew me.*

CHAPTER 5

THE SAWMILL

Thirty minutes later, she saw Cousin Melvin approaching. He stood in the yard and asked her if she wanted to tour the mill site with him.

"Guests at the hotel will be asking questions about the mill, and I want you to have some of the answers," Melvin said. Bennie knew she must follow Mr. Knox's advice and learn about Helen if she was going to serve restaurant guests at the town's best hotel.

Maybe Ovaleen doesn't live in Helen. Maybe she's just visiting the town and is leaving today.

She put down her sewing and joined her cousin. They walked down the road and across the wooden covered bridge that spanned the Chattahoochee River. The first thing that caught Bennie's eye was a large pond where logs floated in front of the large, two-story mill building. Cousin Melvin explained how important it was that the logs be washed before entering the mill. Dirt damaged the saws, and if a rock became embedded in a log and wasn't removed, it could cause the saw to disintegrate into sharp flying projectiles.

Ovaleen's talk can contain sharp flying words that leave permanent injuries, Bennie thought.

Melvin continued. Logs were dirty when they were put on the flatcars because the snake crew used mules and oxen to drag the logs from the cutting sites to the railway. The front ends of the logs were placed on metal trays called "lizards" to prevent them from digging into the dirt and to ease the dragging process.

"Oxen drivers and mule drivers argue a lot about which animal is best. The mule can pull the biggest load, but oxen are less expensive to feed," Melvin said.

He explained that the Shay locomotive pulled the loaded flatcars to the pond beside the mill. The railroad track next to the pond was tilted toward the water. After the train stopped, the supporting braces were removed and the logs rolled off into the water.

I wish people could act like braces and keep hurtful words from being spoken.

Bennie silently vowed to stop thinking about Ovaleen, to listen better, and to remember every word Melvin said. She had to know as much as she could about Helen if she wanted to do well in her job.

Men, who held long poles with sharp metal spikes and hooks on the end, were walking at the edge of the pond; now and then, a man walked on the logs. With the poles, they turned the logs to examine every inch and then guided them onto a conveyor belt that went up to the second floor of the mill. "Those poles are called peaveys," Melvin said. Water sprayed the logs again after they were on the conveyor.

The Helen sawmill is putting trees into a pool before changing them into perfectly shaped, useful lumber. I've come to Helen to put my daughter into a school. I hope school will shape her into a learned child. That will be useful for us both.

Men were working on the second-floor window where the logs went into the mill. "They're making that opening bigger," said Melvin. "We have a big poplar log with a butt seven feet wide. It was one hundred twenty-five feet high, straight as a gun barrel, and it's too big to go through without enlarging the opening. It's going to be sawed into two-inch planks, four feet wide and six feet long. After these planks are dried and planed, they'll be shipped to a company for staining and heavy varnishing. They'll become business conference tables, and we have an order from a company in New York for all we can produce."

"These mountains are covered in a wonderful virgin forest," Bennie said. *A virgin forest, like a virgin woman, hasn't been explored by man.* After learning some of the country's history, she thought some of the trees in Spring Cove were older than America.

She couldn't think about trees without remembering that her father used only four trees to build their log cabin. When she became old enough, Bennie had handled one end of the crosscut saw to help him cut wood for burning in the kitchen stove and fireplace. She pulled the saw toward her, and he pulled the saw toward him. If either one pushed, the rhythm was lost. Later she and her mother slowly developed the same pull-pull rhythm. They cut smaller hardwoods, but it still was hard work.

"The orders for lumber don't stop coming. We had a gold rush here in north Georgia; now we have a timber rush. People can get rich either way," Melvin said, chuckling.

"What is being done with so much lumber?" Bennie said.

"Wood is necessary for anything a man does—for buildings, for boxes, for heating and cooking, for everything," Melvin said.

Jobs were plentiful at the mill because wood was necessary throughout the country, literally from the cradle to the coffin. Food was the first life-supporting commodity, and wood was second. Not only was wood the main source of heating fuel used in stoves and fireplaces, but it also was made into buildings, barrels, buckets, furniture, wagons, farm tools, silos, and more. Trees were needed for ships, railroad ties, railway cars, and frames for the noisy new motor cabs with petrol engines.

Previously, wood from the South had been considered soft and inferior because the trees grew faster and had not survived hard winters. Stumpland— more than thirty-one million acres where trees once stood in Michigan, Minnesota, and Wisconsin—was causing the South to gain dominance in the timber industry, and the Georgia mountain forests were thick and plentiful.

Large mills and plants in the South were built by non-southerners. It was as if the exploitation, which gave Yankees the name of carpetbaggers or scalawags during the Reconstruction era, was continuing. Fifty years had passed since the North beat the South in the War between the States, but deep resentment for northerners still existed.

Governments in southern states passed laws making life more difficult for black freedmen, and the government in Washington, DC, passed laws preventing southern states from exporting goods. The South was poor and had no money for investment, such as that required by a big sawmill.

Successful midwestern businessmen heard about the valuable standing timber in northeast Georgia from a man who made his living as a timber cruiser. Such cruisers traveled all the states looking for large acreage with standing timber and then acted as brokers for logging investors. The cruiser reported poplar trees measuring twenty to thirty feet in circumference, and thousands of trees fifty to sixty feet high before a limb was seen. They were chestnuts, oaks, maples, wild cherries, walnut, mahogany, and more. The area was rich in trees and poor in business knowledge.

Farming the steep mountain hillsides was out of the question, and the midwesterners purchased thirty-six thousand acres of land in northeast Georgia for a song. Using the valuable virgin timber as collateral, they formed an investment company, obtained loans from Missouri banks, and built the giant sawmill, village, and railroad. It transformed the silent, peaceful little valley north of the larger Nacoochee Valley into a noisy rough-and-tumble town.

Melvin again talked about his job assisting the sawmill manager. "One of the most important things we have to do is make sure the right amount of good logs are coming into the mill, enough to keep it steadily operating, but not so many logs that we have to find a storage place for them. It's not easy. One poplar tree made so many logs that it completely filled all the train's flatcars."

He pointed to the field of perfectly stacked lumber, every piece in each stack the exact same size, and every stack the exact same height and width. They could see only the beginning row, which was higher than their heads, and to Bennie, it resembled the edge of a giant honeycomb. It stretched between the road and the river, and Melvin said the stacks covered five acres.

"The stackers must be honest, dedicated men. They accurately mark the lumber and are careful that it avoids warping and twisting. It will stay here for drying, sometimes for nine months, and then it goes into the heated kiln until the water content is no more than two percent. That can take from one to three months, depending on the age of the tree."

In all that he explained, Melvin didn't mention how hard the work was and its dangers. Cutting a tree required strong, hearty men. First they used axes to cut a good-sized notch in the tree near the ground. Next, two men pulled a long crosscut saw back and forth in the notch. The saw was sometimes called a whipsaw because it was flexible, and the man on each end had to know how to keep it steady.

The felling crew tried to make the tree hit the ground in a specific location away from other trees and other life. A tree that fell on a man or work animal meant instant death or permanent injury. Although many of the workers had no experience as woods hicks, no one had been seriously injured.

The felling crew also made sure that the snaking or skidding crew would not have to drag trees or logs uphill.

He didn't explain the difficult construction of the train track spurs, or the dirty work of removing the rails and muddy ties when the work was finished at one of the locations. He didn't tell Bennie that the log train, when returning to the camps, had to be loaded with wholesome, energy-producing food for the men, as well as hay, oats, and yellow corn for the mules and oxen. Saw filers and farriers, experts in their fields, also rode the train to the camps. The saws and axes had to be constantly filed and sharpened, and farriers took care of the animals' feet. Both mules and oxen had to have good iron shoes and properly trimmed hooves.

Cousin Melvin also didn't mention the swamping crew that had to clear felled trees of their branches or the bucking crew that cut the felled trees, sometimes called boles, into logs. Then the loading crew moved the logs onto the flatcars.

He stopped Bennie before they entered the noisy mill to explain what she was going to see. The logs entered the mill on the conveyor belt, were dumped onto a deck, and from there were fastened to a carriage, which traveled on tracks. The carriage moved the log into the band saw, a shiny, whirling metal loop eight feet long and ten inches wide with sharp teeth, which sawed off the outside slab with the bark. After the first slab was removed, the carriage went back to the deck, and men rolled over the log for another side to be sawed. Men wearing shields, which protected their faces from flying debris, rode the carriage and positioned the logs. "It's extremely risky work," Melvin said. They were still about fifty yards from the mill, and he spoke loudly to be heard above the noise.

Cleaned of the bark, the square log was called a cant. The cant was pushed onto another carriage that took it to the gang saw. The gang saw had several blades set at exact intervals that changed the cant into boards with one swipe. The new boards moved into a group of small circular saws called edgers and lost any uneven edges with bark. After the edgers, another group of circular saws did the trimming or squared the ends.

"One man is in a control booth. He's called a sawyer. He makes sure the log is set properly and the saws remain steady," Melvin said. He was talking about the sawmill with great pride, as if he was the one responsible for its success.

After they stepped inside the mill, the noise was unbearable and Bennie slapped both hands tightly over her ears. The band saw was making a shrill screech, and the other saws were making loud noises that sounded almost like heavy groans. At the same time, the five steam engines in the building next door were hissing and throbbing as they operated the generators that produced electricity.

In addition to the hellish noise, the air was hot and humid. Bennie could see that the shirt of every man was wet with sweat.

Some of the men were marking the planks and loading them onto a large cart. Another man apparently was repairing one of the circular saws. After they left the noise of the mill, Melvin said the man working on the saw was a millwright, who was responsible for making sure the machinery was well maintained. "The millwright comes into work each day about an hour before the others just to check the machinery, and we have a shop where saws are filed, as well as a crew that sweeps away all the sawdust and makes sure all the machinery is clean and properly oiled."

Bennie knew she couldn't remember all the details, but she was gaining an understanding about how the sawmill changed tall forests into stacks of raw planks in uniform sizes. She planned to make notes that evening about the whole operation.

After she and Melvin went back across the bridge, Dorothy invited them to have an apple with store-bought peanut butter and soda crackers. She again invited Bennie and Kat to supper that evening. "Thank you. I'm beginning work tomorrow, and we'll start eating at the restaurant," Bennie said.

CHAPTER 6

THE RESTAURANT

At Mrs. Ross's house, Bennie found three laughing children huddled over a wooden box containing puppies while Mrs. Ross sat on her steps and watched.

Bennie told Mrs. Ross she would be working in the hotel six days a week and asked if she could bring Kat to her house before five o'clock each morning.

"Ya kin bring 'er in 'n' put'er to sleep on the settee," Mrs. Ross said, adding that she could keep Kat for fifty cents a week. "N' ah hope ya can bring us some leftover food from the hotel kitchen."

Throughout the evening, Bennie thought about going to work the next morning, and when the alarm clock went off at quarter past four, she was already awake. After she put her new white apron over a dark blue dress, she helped Kat get dressed, lit her lantern, and walked her to Mrs. Ross's.

As she walked to the hotel, Bennie was thankful that Kat had a good place to stay. Mr. Knox took her to the kitchen just as the company's five o'clock whistle blew. "Bennie Sheldon, meet Herbert Gale. Herb, Miz Sheldon's here to work in the kitchen, whatever ya want 'er to do."

The tall, skinny man standing at the table with a knife in his hand turned and looked at Bennie. "Was Benjamin Sheldon yore daddy?" Herbert Gale said. When Bennie said yes, he said, "He took my papa's place at the cheese factory. Papa liked 'im a lot." He was referring to the small goat cheese factory at the foot of Tray Mountain where Bennie's father had worked before it closed.

Herb Gale was slicing ham on a large table, and he gestured toward a woman near him who was sifting flour. Her skin was the color of caramel. A faded blue cloth was wrapped around her head, and a white apron covered her faded, darker blue dress. "This here's Fannie Mae," he said. "Jus' stay close 'n' watch what we're doin' today, and tomorrow I'll give ya jobs to do."

Bennie looked toward the woman and had to force her gaze away before it became a stare. She didn't know what to say. She had never before seen such a dark-skinned person, but her mother had told her many stories about slavery, her colored friends from Africa, and the War between the States that ended slavery. She knew her father left his family's rice plantation after the slaves were freed and Union soldiers burned the main buildings, but he never talked about it.

While Bennie was trying to think what she could say to Fannie Mae, another man came in. "Fresh from the farm," he said, putting gallon glass jars of milk on the table. Herb explained that the man came from the Hardman Farm about two miles away. Bennie recalled words from Williams, the peddler, who said he didn't understand how the mountain terrain with its scarce population could have attracted the sawmill and the dairy farm, two business ventures of record size, in one small mountainous area. "That's tha rezin they built a train to Gainesville. They kin take the lumber and milk, too, to people who need 'em," he said.

Herb pointed to a large shiny container on a side table. "I know what ya kin do. Fill that kin two-thirds fulla water 'n' we'll make coffee. You'll find roasted coffee beans 'n' a grinder over there, 'n' you'll need a full cuppa grounds."

Bennie felt as if she was groping in the dark, but she did as instructed and hoped that her actions would produce the coffee he wanted.

An hour passed before she realized it, and Izzy Gale, a heavyset woman whom Herb introduced as his wife, motioned for Bennie to accompany her. She showed Bennie the restaurant's toilet, explaining that the sink had hot and cold running water.

Mrs. Gale asked Bennie to accompany her again as she seated two men. After taking their orders, Bennie got silver utensils and stared in wonder at the ornate "M" on each handle, designating the Mountain Hotel's ownership.

More guests arrived, all men, and asked for eggs and either bacon or ham. One man asked for fried souse meat, a meat jelly made from the flesh of a hog head and sometimes called headcheese. Mrs. Gale told Bennie that more people would come in for the noon meal called dinner, which decades later was called lunch, and supper, the evening meal.

After serving the customers, Bennie dried dishes, pots, and pans while Fannie Mae washed. Neither woman spoke until they were almost finished. Then, keeping her eyes lowered, Fannie Mae said, "How long ya been here?" Bennie felt relieved to be able to answer her question.

After learning that Bennie had come from Tray Mountain only two days earlier, Fannie Mae asked about the rest of her family and learned that her parents were dead.

"Ya bin livin' by yerself?"

"No, I have a daughter. We came here so she could go to school."

"Ya musta married young. Ah guess yo' man's young as you."

Bennie said, "Katherine's father left us before she was born." Her expression caused Fannie Mae to become quiet again.

The noon meal came and went with food the only thing changing. Again all the diners were men. Before time for the evening meal, the tables were covered with beautiful snow-white linen cloths. A woman brought in clusters of wild flowers to put in small vases for the tables. A loud bell rang to signify that supper was ready, and some of the men at the evening meal were accompanying women.

Bennie learned her simple duties quickly, and Mrs. Gale didn't come into the dining area the next day. Katherine was happy at Mrs. Ross's house, and Bennie got permission to take each day's leftover biscuits and cornbread to her. Herb told her to also take the syrup bottle that had an inch of thick sorghum left in the bottom.

Five days passed, and new guests arrived on Saturday. Bennie was becoming relaxed enough in her duties that she was able to admire the women's clothing. Some wore gold watch-bracelets, which fascinated her.

She was shocked on Saturday evening when she went to pick up Katherine at Mrs. Ross's house.

"Mr. Bristol's in Helen for the weeken'. He's Hank and Goldie's daddy, and he said he can't let his chil'ren play with yore girl," Mrs. Ross said.

Bennie's heart raced, and she stared at Mrs. Ross without speaking. After a minute, she turned and went into the yard to get Kat where the children were playing with the puppies again.

Mrs. Ross hurried behind and put a hand on Bennie's arm to delay her. "I don' wanna do this. Hank and Goldie's daddy said their mama spoke from heaven, tellin' 'im to move 'is chil'ren."

Bennie couldn't bear to hear any more, and she walked away, pulling Katherine by the hand. *Ovaleen Birch didn't waste any time. My child is only five years old and completely innocent.* Kat would be deeply hurt because she couldn't return to play with Hank and Goldie.

As they went toward their room, Kat said, "Mama, why are you walking so fast?" Inside, Bennie told Katherine to go to bed and wait while she went to the hotel. Katherine didn't make another sound. She had never seen her mother so upset.

At the hotel, Bennie didn't see Knox so she went straight to the kitchen. Herb was outside the back door smoking a hand-rolled cigarette and talking to a woods hick. As he stepped inside the door, Bennie said stiffly, "Mr. Gale, I can't work here anymore." Her face was bright red.

"What's the matter?" Herb said.

"Mrs. Ross can't keep Katherine anymore."

Herb didn't know what to say. He knew that Mr. Knox wanted Bennie to work in the restaurant. He looked at Bennie, then at the floor, and then looked at her again. Bennie started to leave, but he said, "Wait. Jes' bring yore girl ta the kitchen with ya, and maybe ya kin find sumpun to keep 'er busy."

"But we can't keep coming here. Guests will object to me and my daughter," Bennie said.

"Yore a good worker. I want ya here. Bring yore lit'l girl and come back in tha mornin'."

Bennie was silent a minute, and then she thanked him. She promised to continue working and left the kitchen with her thoughts in turmoil. *I should go back home, but I can't. Katherine must go to school.* She tried to think of how she would tell Katherine of the change. She couldn't tell a child that others thought her mere presence was a bad influence.

Back in their room, Bennie told Kat that she wouldn't be going to Mrs. Ross's house anymore. Kat only looked silently at her mother with wide questioning eyes. The world in Helen was too different and strange for her to object. Her mother also was acting strange. "Mrs. Ross is a good woman, and I know how you like Hank and Goldie, but I need you to go to work with me."

Young Kat continued to stare at her mother. "We'll take your new Blue Horse tablet, and you can write your ABCs and numbers. I want you to begin learning more multiplication tables and do arithmetic too. You've got to be ready for school."

"Hank and Goldie have been teaching me," Kat said.

"That's good, but you are my daughter. We have to stay together, and when you're in the kitchen with me, you can watch me work with other people. You may have to do the same kind of work someday."

Bennie really wasn't convinced that she still had a job. "I'm going to do the best I can, and I want you to do the best you can to get ready for school," she said as they began undressing.

Sleep escaped Bennie that night as she tried to prepare her mind for more rejections. *Who is going to be next, and what if they make hateful remarks to Katherine? How will I explain such actions to my sweet girl? What can I do to protect her? I wish I could take her back home.*

CHAPTER 7

CHURCHED

Despite Bennie's anxiety, Kat adapted to her new surroundings in the hotel restaurant as easy as she had adapted to Mrs. Ross's care. She found every action interesting because she had never known people other than her mother, grandparents, and the Rigsbys, and she was totally awed by the large kitchen.

Bennie placed one of the large metal pots upside down on the floor, placed the tablet and pencil on top, and Katherine sat down beside it so she could use it for her table. But she was too curious about her surroundings to write anything on her tablet. She looked around to watch what was happening and couldn't stop staring at Fannie Mae.

That evening, she said, "How did Miss Fannie Mae get so brown?" Bennie reminded her how Nana had talked about the woman who looked after her when she was a child. "Nana's parents owned colored people like Fannie Mae. Her ancestors were captured and brought from Africa to work as slaves. Slaves were bought and owned by rich people. They had to work for the owners. All slaves were set free after the war. Remember, Nana told you about the War between the States and how the Union Army captured her father. Fannie Mae's own mama probably was a slave," Bennie said.

When they arrived the second morning, Kat began writing diligently. Her tongue moved from one corner of her lips to the other as she concentrated. She got up and talked to her mother while she was drying dishes, and that afternoon she put her head on her arms on top of the pot and slept for two hours.

The next day, Bennie found an issue of the *Grit*, "America's Greatest Family Newspaper," left on a table, and gave it to Kat, who began copying the words. She found an advertisement picturing a beautiful woman with an abundance of hair coming around her shoulders, and took the paper to Bennie. "Mama, this looks like you when you brush your hair," she said.

"You can draw that woman. You're good with art," Bennie said. Kat was going quickly through the tablet, and Bennie told her she would have to use both sides of the paper.

Herb and Izzy Gale lived only a few yards behind the hotel, and Izzy sometimes came to the kitchen and invited Katherine to come and play with the Gales' children, a ten-year-old daughter, Abby; an eight-year-old son, Junior; and a two-year-old son, Matthew.

Days passed, and Bennie learned that the teacher had arrived and was available to talk about the coming school year. She had rehearsed her expected conversation with the teacher so much that she thought about it in her sleep. She was preparing to beg, something she had never done before. Whatever happened, Kat must not begin school and then be forced out. Such an action would completely destroy all pleasures in the young girl's life.

She waited until midmorning, anxiously left the kitchen, and walked to the small one-room school. The teacher, the only person in the room, got up from her desk to welcome Bennie. "I'm Miss Tatum," she said.

Bennie didn't think of introducing herself and said, "I want my daughter to come to school."

"How old is she?"

"She's five years old. She knows her ABCs, can count to one hundred, and can recite her twos and threes multiplication tables. She's been practicing writing and is excited about coming to school."

"She'll be welcome. She should bring a pencil and a writing tablet."

Bennie wasn't concerned that she would have to buy another new tablet. "But I must tell you now, if she starts to school, she must continue. I don't want her to be thrown out," she said.

"Why would she be thrown out?"

"She's a woods colt, a woods child," Bennie said, using mountain terminology to describe a shameful condition.

Miss Tatum paused and then said, "I'll welcome her."

Bennie was silent a few seconds before she said, "You mean she can come to your school?"

"Absolutely."

Bennie still was ready to beg and couldn't believe there was no need. "Thank you. Thank you," she finally said. Miss Tatum asked her name and her daughter's name before saying she would look forward to having Katherine as a student.

As Bennie walked back to the hotel, she thought about how she would leave Kat in bed and ask Cousin Dorothy to wake her two hours later to go to the restaurant for breakfast and then to school.

Suddenly she noticed that the sky was bright blue, the air was clear, the trees had started to develop beautiful autumn colors, and the mountains were beckoning. *When did everything become so beautiful?* For the first time, she thought that the new mountain town was an exciting place. She looked toward the sky. *I'm still in the mountains, Mama, and Kat's going to school.*

An excited Katherine began school. Following her mother's instructions, she went to the hotel kitchen during breaks for recess and lunch. She also went there immediately when school was out.

Bennie was enjoying welcoming guests to the dining room and serving the tables. Once, while she was explaining an order to Herb, Bennie saw Izzy glaring at her as if she had uttered a vulgarity. *Izzy knows, and she doesn't want me here,* she thought.

Katherine's question one evening surprised Bennie although she had been trying to prepare proper words if the subject was mentioned. Her daughter had been especially quiet in the hotel kitchen and on the way to their room. After they were preparing for bed, she said, "Mama, can I ask you something?"

"Of course, sugar."

"Did it hurt when they churched you?"

Bennie could not answer for a minute. Then she said, "It hurt my heart."

"Did you bleed?"

"No, honey. Do you remember how sad you were when Nana died? That's because your heart was hurting. That's what I meant. My heart was hurting because I was very, very sad. Being churched means that I was told I couldn't go to Sunday school and preaching anymore. I couldn't see my friends, and it made me cry."

"Why did that happen?"

"The people in the church said I made a mistake with my life. Let's not worry because it happened a long time ago. They couldn't stop me from loving Jesus. That's why you and I pray to God through Jesus's name every day."

"Hank and Goldie said they can't play with me because you were churched, and I'm a woods colt."

"If they're not playing with you, they are missing one of the sweetest girls in the first grade. Other students will be your friends."

Before Katherine could speak again, Bennie kissed her and said, "I hope you have sweet dreams."

Bennie had started keeping a journal and wrote in the mornings while Kat still slept. The next morning, her first written words were "I hope my little girl never has to suffer a broken heart."

CHAPTER 8

TRAVELING PREACHER

The loud work whistle continued to blast its signals, and the passenger/freight train continued to chug-a-lug into town morning and evening, screaming its arrival. The Shay engine continued to rat-a-tat up to the pond to unload its logs, and the freight train left again with stacks of lumber chained to its flatcars. As weeks passed, Bennie stopped being aware of the loud sounds as she became interested in what the hotel guests were saying.

"Sawmilling is the best way to make a pile of money" was a remark she heard more than once. Talk about work inside the mill began to fascinate her.

"He has to stand there all day, and it's so hot in there the sweat runs down into his shoes and then puddles out on the floor," said one.

"He wears earplugs and uses hand signals because the noise is so loud they can't talk to each other," said another.

All the guests began talking about a second band saw that was to be added to the mill's operation. That would mean twice as many logs coming in to produce twice as much lumber. She often heard, "Two band saws mean 125,000 board feet a day when the mill is in full operation." The "board foot" measurement referred to a piece of green lumber one foot long, one foot wide, and one inch thick. A small sawmill operation run by a single man could produce 100 board feet a day. It was estimated that 125,000 board feet could be taken from a poplar tree 225 feet high, 48 feet around, and more than 15 feet in diameter, with the first limb at 90 feet.

Cousin Dorothy and Cousin Melvin sometimes came to the restaurant for the evening meal, and they always asked Bennie to join them at the Haydens' for Bible study on Sunday. Other guests offered to pick up her and Katherine on Sunday morning to attend a church in Nacoochee Valley. She always declined, but an unusual event in Helen found her at a church service.

It happened when a traveling preacher set up his tent beside the river for revival services. Early in the morning after the preacher's arrival, his son, sixteen or seventeen years old, was helping erect the tent when he was struck by lightning and killed. The body was stretched on the ground while the preacher continued work as if nothing had happened. With two younger children and two volunteers, he unloaded an old piano plus planks that made wooden benches and arranged them under the tent.

It was late September, but the weather had been unusually hot. Thunderclouds had gathered the day before and produced flashes of lightning and a hard, quick rain. Bennie had never heard of lightning killing anyone, although she had seen a huge tree split down the center. She had heard comments recently about how people should get off the telephone during storms, but she didn't worry because she wasn't going to use a telephone.

The revival preacher announced he was going to do divine healings and bring his son back to life. Seats would be available for one hundred people. The young man's body was moved to a front bench near the piano, and services began at seven o'clock. People were hesitant to go, but they also were curious. The tent was half full on the first night.

The preacher's wife played the piano, and the preacher, wearing a white jacket that emphasized his longish black hair, led the group in the song, *Shall We Gather at the River*, emphasizing the words "flowing by the throne of God." Holding a thick Bible in his left hand, he pounded it and said, "God is present in this tent, and you can be saved. I'll baptize you here in the wonderful Chattahoochee

River. You must repent of your sins and leave your evil ways. While we are here, I want everyone to see a marvelous healing and witness the glory of God. That's why my son, Walter, is on the front bench. I want you to see him rise up after God heals him. That's why he was struck by lightning. God wants you to see what he alone can do," he said.

On the second night, people who couldn't find a seat were standing across the back. They wanted to be there when the son came back to life.

The preacher and other men took turns sitting beside the body, two through each day and night, and the body was covered with a sheet that was removed during each service.

The standing crowd grew larger on the third night, and the preacher shed tears as he said attendants were failing to repent, and that was the reason his son wasn't returning to life. On the fifth night, the body was bloated and an odor was developing. People still were going in at meeting time because the preacher told them it was God's wishes. Because they thought the young man might actually get up, they sat only on the benches away from the front and stood in the back. How long was this going to continue? What was going to happen?

Bennie was working and wished she could attend the service when Izzy came in. She said she wasn't going to the services anymore and would relieve Bennie so she could attend. Surprised but grateful for Izzy's offer, Bennie grabbed Katherine by the hand and they both found standing room in the tent. Every person "who believes in God" was asked to come forward, touch the boy's head, and pray for their own repentance and the boy's new life. Most of the people had not had a good look at him, and the boy's eyes still were open as well as his mouth. They filed slowly past him, barely touching his cheek. Three people were in line ahead of Bennie, when a man spread his hand, put his palm on the boy's forehead, pressed it, and tried to shake him. When he did, a green fly flew out of the boy's mouth. The woman walking beside the man squealed and swooned. The next man caught her before she fell to the ground. Young Katherine and Bennie grabbed each other and didn't move.

After this happened, no one else approached the body until the preacher told them they were not obeying God's wishes. Bennie, Kat, and everyone still in line filed past silently and reached down with their index finger, but did not actually touch the boy.

Everybody in Helen was thinking about the preacher and his son. What was going to happen to that dead boy?

As the clock approached seven-thirty on the sixth evening, the sheriff and two men from the nearby town of Cleveland went into the tent, one man carrying a stretcher. The sheriff said, "This body is gonna spread disease."

The preacher refused to let them approach the body, saying he was going to begin having services both morning and evening "and God will prevail." The sheriff pulled his gun, pointed it toward the man, and said, "I'm sorry you lost your son, but we got to bury this body."

The two men grabbed the preacher and handcuffed him. The preacher's wife screamed, ran to her husband, and wrapped her arms around him, but one of the men pulled her away. The preacher's other children, who had been sitting on the same bench as their dead brother, never moved. The men then rolled the boy's body onto the stretcher, put it on a wagon, and left, traveling toward Cleveland.

Words heard later were "I guess that preacher musta been living wrong. That's why lightning killed his son." Like all others in Helen, Bennie and Fannie Mae talked about it. They heard that the body had been buried in a Cleveland churchyard, and the preacher had him dug up the next day. People assumed that the preacher had him buried closer to his home.

"I guess the preacher really believed his son would come back to life," Bennie said.

"I guess Jesus healed him a'ter he got to heaven," Fannie Mae said. "He 'as healed and free then."

Herb added, "Tha preacher musta got anuf money 'cause he was passin' the basket ever' night and scared some of tha people 'til they parted with more dollers than they do at usual preachin'."

Suddenly Bennie remembered something her mother said back when Bennie was banned from church. "People pick words out of the Bible that supports what they want to do," Marie said. "A person can always find words that condemn another's actions or supports their own behavior. Just remember 'God is love.'"

Preachers don't always know what God wants. That preacher found words supporting what he needed. Believing in healing power relieved him from heartbreak about his dead son, Bennie thought. *He didn't win anyone to belief in Jesus, but maybe he'll be recognized for effort in God's book of life.*

CHAPTER 9

THE STRANGER

One morning, Bennie took a second look at the stranger who walked in for breakfast. He had on a cream-colored shirt, a narrow black string tie, and khaki pants, and he was holding a dark felt hat in his hand. Mountain people didn't wear the khaki color, and something about his clean-shaven face was different. *He looks happy. He must have just settled an important deal.*

Guests were almost always officers with the sawmill company or other businessmen intent in their conversations with one another or anxiously watching for someone, hoping to close a deal.

When she welcomed the stranger with intentions to seat him, his blue eyes stared into her brown eyes as if she were a dear friend he hadn't seen in a long time. She thought he was going to say something to her, but he didn't speak. She seated him beside one of the windows.

"May I take your order?" she said, trying not to feel uncomfortable. He was staring but lowered his eyes and ordered. "Sweet milk with eggs, grits, and bacon." (Milk had not yet been homogenized, so everyone in the Deep South said "sweet milk" to refer to whole milk without the cream removed to make butter and buttermilk.)

"May I bring you coffee?" she said.

"No, it makes me jittery," he said and smiled up at her. *I wonder if his eyes make everything look blue to him,* Bennie thought, smiling to herself.

He had finished his breakfast and was leaving when Bennie collected the money for his meal. He introduced himself. "I'm Caleb Alexander. I've been invited here to help organize a church. We're having meetings each Sunday in the home of Mr. and Mrs. Hayden, and I hope you'll join us."

Oh, he's a preacher.

Bennie thanked him for the invitation but didn't introduce herself. She knew that her cousins attended the services at the Hayden home. She also knew she was not welcome at a church.

Immediately after breakfast, Mr. Knox called the hotel staff together. He told them that *The Constitution*, a newspaper in Atlanta, was organizing a motor party to travel to Helen and stay in their hotel for five days.

It was October, and automobile tourism was reaching the Georgia mountains. Leisure travel had always been a luxury of wealthy people who traveled in ships or trains to distant, exotic places and stayed for months. The growing popularity of motorcars meant tourists could travel only a few hours or a couple of days to an alluring place if the roads were passable.

Such short leisure travel was new and rare; roads had no guidance signs at all, no assistance was available if motorcars became disabled, and gasoline had to be purchased at pharmacies. The Atlanta organizers of the ninety-mile trip to Helen planned to use the newspaper's radio station and two engineering students from the Georgia Institute of Technology to report progress back to the Atlanta public. The students would carry with them the institute's mobile radio equipment, which filled the backseat of one car. They would have to make sure the radio broadcast reached the Atlanta audience, and they would have to perform repairs on the caravan's five motorcars.

The letter announcing the plans came on the morning train, and Knox sent a welcoming reply to the newspaper that same day. The group was to include a famous Atlanta millionaire and his wife, plus five other couples, the organizer, and the two Georgia technology students—fifteen people in all. They were expected to arrive on Friday of the following week, twelve days away.

Knox said the train would deliver cases of the new bottled drink, Coca-Cola, enough to supply the guests throughout their stay. The millionaire, who was part of the traveling group, owned the company that sold the fizzy new drink.

"We must do everythin' we kin to make sure these folks go back 'n' tell their frien's to come visit us, too," Knox said. His excitement was obvious, and he asked the staff to listen as he read portions of the newspaper article that came with the letter. The printed words said the hotel was in the most beautiful mountain setting, and the topsoil roads leading to Helen were so good that the cars could average thirty-five miles per hour.

"An older Atlanta news story said the Nacoochee Valley was 'the Garden of Eden,' and tha's the reason air hotel was built here. It's so visitors kin enjoy the beauty," Knox said.

Hotel and restaurant staff began cleaning diligently each day before the expected arrival. Although the hotel was new, its condition was so important to Mr. Knox that he regularly rubbed a white-gloved hand on shelves, banisters, and even the overhead light fixtures in each room to find dust. The inside of the hotel was cleaned the first week with plans to clean everything outside during the second week before the guests' arrival.

Excitement overflowed in the hotel staff and spread throughout the little town. The excitement Bennie was experiencing left her feeling confident and somewhat daring. Her new life in Helen was a surprising adventure.

Before the announcement of the important visitors, Bennie took a half hour off in midmorning and again in midafternoon. Her half-hour breaks stopped when the hotel was being cleaned, but she still did not have to report to work on Monday, her day off.

On the Monday before the Atlanta guests arrived, she was restless. During the morning, she washed dresses, drawers, and aprons before hanging them to dry on the backyard clothesline. In the afternoon, she decided to leave her room and explore Helen. The weather with its nippy inviting air was too beautiful to resist. The autumn trees were beckoning. She had to get outside. She had no idea such an action was forbidden.

Back in Spring Cove, she sometimes walked up to a rock overlook where she could sit and drink in the majesty of the rolling mountaintops. She told her mother she was celebrating the mountains because the view always refreshed her thoughts and brightened her day. If she found a nice place to walk in Helen, she and Kat could go together later.

She put on her cotton gloves and bonnet, walked to the bridge, crossed it, and discovered a path following the river. Men working at the pond stopped to stare at her, and one of them sent a wolf whistle her way. She wondered if such a short whistle signaled something wrong with a log, turned to look at the men, didn't see a problem, and walked on.

She felt brave and curious. Large red and yellow trees shaded the footpath while vines, moss, and other wild growth lined each side of the path in greenery. She enjoyed looking at bright red or yellow leaves that had fallen along the path, and the farther she walked, the more free she felt.

Eventually she arrived at a four-story building with a sign that said Nora Mill Granary. Her daddy had talked about the granary years ago, and she knew that it had large stones that slowly ground corn into meal or grits and wheat into flour.

She didn't go to the front of the corn mill but sat down behind the granary beside a small dam in the river. She had not enjoyed sitting in solitude and connecting with nature since arriving in Helen. The smooth splashing sound of water pouring over the dam filled her mind with peace, making her totally free of apprehension for the first time since she left Spring Cove. Beside the riverbank, the water was mirror smooth and clear as glass. After looking at fish moving about, she leaned forward and put her fingers in the water, finding it cold and refreshing. *I wonder why our mountain water is always so cold?*

"Good afternoon, Miss. I see you're enjoying this beautiful day," said a male voice behind her.

She jumped to her feet and whirled around. It was Caleb Alexander who had come to Helen to organize a church.

"Oh, hello," he said after he saw her face. "I'm sorry. I didn't mean to startle you."

"I must go back. My daughter will be coming home," she said.

"I have to return too. I'll escort you," he said.

Bennie had already started walking and didn't answer him. He began walking behind her.

"You can call me Caleb. I don't know your name," he said.

"I'm Bennie Sheldon," she said, still walking ahead and not daring to look back toward him. His presence made her very aware. Her whole body was tingling, telling her to get away from him.

"Do you live near the hotel?" he said.

"Yes."

"I'm staying there until I can find another room somewhere," he said.

She walked faster.

"Remember? I'm here to organize a church, and I hope you can come and worship with us on Sunday."

"I have to work on Sunday." She didn't tell him she took a break at midmorning.

"We also have a short Bible study service each Wednesday evening. Maybe you can join us then."

"I have to work on Wednesday evening too."

Bennie didn't know she had walked so far from her room. Walking past the small lake where men with peaveys were rolling the logs, he said, "I'm glad I found you and could escort you back to your home. I hope I'll see you again." Finally she arrived at her cousin's house with Alexander close behind.

I must be hospitable where the hotel's business is concerned, Bennie thought. She turned toward him, lifted her hand in a half-wave, and said, "I'll see you when you come for meals."

She was deeply frustrated as she walked up the steps and entered her room. *He ruined my day.*

Kat came home from school, and Bennie had forgotten her agitation. She was excited about the fact that she had gone somewhere alone, other than to the hotel. She told Kat about the wonderful path she found beside the river. "The Chattahoochee River is beautiful, and Nana said rivers are the elixir of life. Towns grow beside rivers, and a walk beside the river can lift our spirits. We'll walk down it together after school on my next day off."

They were leaving the house to go to the hotel kitchen for supper when Cousin Melvin stopped them.

"Someone told me you were out walking today without an escort," he said to Bennie.

"I see other women walking without escorts, and I walked beside the river."

Melvin dropped his voice to a whisper. "But you must not walk alone. Those other women you see walking without escorts live at the Commercial Hotel. They entertain woods hicks every weekend, and, forgive me for saying this, but they are unfortunate women. They are prostitutes."

Bennie's face turned bright red, and she finally said, "I didn't know."

"You cannot walk around alone," Melvin said, pausing before each word for emphasis.

"I won't do it again," Bennie said.

Bennie had never before heard the word "prostitute," but she remembered what Ellie Rigsby said. "That new place, Helen, ain't nothin' but devil-may-care men, rotgut whiskey, and bad women." That remark was one reason that Bennie dreaded moving to Helen.

Caleb Alexander had followed Bennie home from the granary with Bennie feeling like he ruined her day. But that was nothing compared to the way Melvin's words made her feel. The walk beside the river opened another door in her life, but now it was slammed shut. *I wish I could talk to Ellie.*

CHAPTER 10

ATLANTA TOURISTS

Only four days remained before the arrival of the Atlanta tourists, and like the rest of the hotel staffers, Bennie began to think of nothing else. During more preparation, the hotel's horses, which were rented to people who wanted to ride the ridges around the Chattahoochee River, were bathed and brushed; the walkways, swimming pool, tennis courts, shuffleboard, and fountain were cleaned. Someone groaned that they had cleaned all the tennis balls as well as the shuffleboard paddles and pucks. Another responded that they might have to clean the goldfish in the fountain.

The words caused Bennie to laugh out loud, and Mr. Knox called her aside. "While our Atlanta guests are here, I hope ya kin smile and laugh more'n ya have been," he said. Bennie had expected a reprimand and smiled at him before she turned away, showing a line of beautiful white teeth without the dark cavities that sometimes blemished the smiles of mountain people. She didn't know her mother's insistence that she always clean her teeth, using the end of a small hickory chewstick as a toothbrush, had given her an advantage. Dentists who filled cavities were rare, expensive, and extremely painful. Tooth extraction, not repairing cavities, was the main form of dentistry.

At about noon on Friday, four motorcars arrived in Helen after stopping for the night at the Princeton Hotel in Gainesville. Two local youths, who heard the cars' noisy approach, ran ahead and breathlessly alerted Mr. Knox before the little caravan crossed the

Chattahoochee River. When the cars began turning into the hotel entrance, the staff was already standing in line on the porch behind Mr. Knox. The guests walked up the steps and stood facing him while he voiced welcoming words and introduced each employee by his or her first name.

Bennie had never seen such beautiful people. She had left her mountain home only three months earlier to come to a new town, and now she felt like she was inside *Harper's Magazine*, the publication her mother had once ordered for three months so Bennie could know about life outside the mountains. The men and women looked exactly like the magazine pictures.

The staffers went back to their work as the guests were escorted to their rooms. All the Atlantans were staying on the main floor, where each room had a private bath with a water toilet. Three young Helen boys, all hired as temporary porters and dressed in white shirts with dark pants, brought the suitcases into the lobby. After they took the luggage to the assigned rooms, they immediately drove a wagon back across the river to the train depot where they found six large trunks containing the names of the guests and addressed to the hotel.

Bennie and Izzy greeted the visitors almost an hour later when they began coming for their midday meal. Bennie was glad that she had no idea which one of the men was the much-discussed millionaire. She had seen the Coca- Cola in brown glass bottles after it was delivered to the hotel and placed in the icebox. She wrote in her journal that Coca-Cola looked like the Fletcher's Castoria medicine her mother once gave her.

The most interesting guests to her were the women who removed their dusters revealing beautiful day dresses. They still were wearing the close- fitting hats that they wore in the motorcars, and some had veils. Bennie hoped she would see them without hats later so she could get an idea about a new way to arrange her hair.

After the guests left, Bennie found coins on four of the tables and reported the finding to Herb. "Tha money's fer you. It's a gratuity, and it means yer a good waitress," he said. Bennie decided she would put the money in her sewing box where she could get it if the guests wanted it back.

After the meal, the guests began standing around the fountain and pond, and both men and women said, "Fishie, fishie," as they tried to attract the goldfish. Mr. Knox took each one a tiny bit of corn bread and told them they could crumble it on the pond to draw the fish close.

During the afternoon, the guests divided their activities between playing horseshoes or tennis and riding horseback along the ridges. Mr. Knox asked if anyone would like to tour the mill on the following day, and all the men signed up. At supper, they asked Bennie how many men had been injured or killed in such hard, dangerous work.

"The sawmill has had no bad injuries. The woods hicks are very careful, and the trees have not been felled on any man, ox, or mule," Bennie said, repeating Cousin Melvin's information.

After supper that evening, a string band played for square dancing, and Helen residents came to dance as always. This time, the local people had dressed to impress the guests, and laughter kept bursting out among the Atlantans as they tried to keep time to the fast music and dance calls.

> Circle eight and you get straight.
> We all go south on the Gainesville freight.
> Knock down Sal and pick up Kate,
> And we all join hands and circle eight.

Bennie found coins again on four of the tables, and she dropped them in her apron pocket until she could put them in her little box with the other coins.

When the guests came for the next meal, Bennie heard the words "two band saws" over and over, and one or two men talked about the cleanliness of the mill. She was glad that she could answer the few questions, but one of the women asked Bennie a question she couldn't answer. "This is one of the most beautiful places I've ever seen. But what will it be like when all the trees are cut?" the woman said.

"I don't know," Bennie said. She had never heard such words. Everyone knew the trees would not all be gone, and the question was foolish.

"Is anyone planting new trees?" the woman asked, and again Bennie said, "I don't know."

The woman said, "With all the trees gone, it will be almost like these beautiful mountains are gone." She then turned to talk to her companions and didn't ask any other questions.

These old mountains will never be without trees. Trees come up all the time, and new ones are growing now. Bennie was remembering the young trees that once grew around their garden. She did not know that clear-cutting was necessary to recoup the major financial investment of a large sawmill, such as the one in Helen. New trees could not grow in a dense forest, and all mature trees capable of reseeding were taken in the clear-cutting process.

She thought of her life as a young girl when she frequently climbed to the top of a tree to see more of the world. She also liked to lay flat on the ground on the many layers of fallen leaves. She could look up at the latticework of limbs and leaves above her and celebrate nature's art. She loved the springtime when the serviceberry tree became a white cloud of delicate blooms, the summer when the white blossoms of the sourwood filled the air with fragrance, and the autumn when the leafy trees and evergreens made the mountains a patchwork quilt of beautiful colors. While the dogwood tree was forever her favorite, she regularly selected other choices. Nothing was more valuable than the wonderful chestnut tree with its sweet treats for people, turkeys, squirrels, and wild boars, and the sugar maples that were both bright red and vivid yellow each fall.

She couldn't imagine life without beautiful, living trees. *I've got too many things to worry about without worrying about trees being gone. The trees can never be gone.*

Each day Bennie learned much about the area around Helen through the activities of the guests and their conversations during the meals.

On Sunday, benches were placed on one of the log train's flatcars. The guests were invited to sit on the benches while the engine slowly chugged them over the hills and across the trestles to one of the woods hicks' camps. They were warned that ashes would be blowing back in the engine smoke, and all the guests wore full-length dusters over their clothes. The women wore the same hats they had on when they arrived in Helen, and some of the men wore the heavy-duty, hickory-striped cotton railroad caps purchased at the Helen commissary. Although the weather was beautiful, every guest was wearing rubber shoes designed for rain and mud. Bennie was amused because some of the women's rubber shoes had stylish "opera toes" and obviously had never been worn.

Before reaching Tray Mountain, the train stopped so the guests could disembark and see Anna Ruby Falls. A path had been formed through the thick rhododendron, mountain laurel, and honeysuckle, and the walk was steep, leaving the hikers out of breath. But upon reaching the double falls, the guests could only exclaim at the beauty. York Creek and Curtis Creek began on Tray Mountain and came together at the top of Anna Ruby Falls to form Smith Creek. The falls were named for the daughter of the man who once owned the surrounding land and who first built the large Nacoochee Valley farm.

On their return to the hotel, the women talked about the beauty of Anna Ruby Falls while the men talked about the houses that were moved, room by room, from one camp to another by train. More than one talked about possible benefits of building rental houses the same way.

On the following day, the group drove their motorcars to Clarkesville and from there to Tallulah Gorge, a deep chasm in rock about two miles long and one thousand feet deep, carved by the simple flowing of a river over millions of years. Two of the Atlanta group had taken the Tallulah Falls train from Cornelia to visit the gorge years earlier. At that time, the Tallulah River was roaring through the gorge, and it was called "The Niagara of the South." After the trip was announced to the group in Helen, the gorge became a main topic of conversation.

Despite strong opposition, construction had just been completed on a hydroelectric dam across the Tallulah River, and a tunnel for the water had been drilled 6,666 feet through solid rock. The tunneled water fell more than 600 feet to turn a giant turbine and generator, which supplied electricity for Atlanta. The fight against the dam put the gorge in the Atlanta news on a regular basis, and some of the hotel's guests supported the water barrier while others opposed it. The visitors wanted to see the results of the dam. At the site, they saw the new lake and stood in the quietness looking into the deep, twisting gorge without its roaring river. They came back from the trip still divided about benefits of the change. Some expressed concern because the dam was causing the old hotels along the gorge's edge to lose their business.

On Wednesday, Knox pulled the hotel staff together once again to bid the guests goodbye. The luggage had been loaded into the cars, and the guests were standing in front of the hotel with the staff on the porch. Knox stood on the steps as he said, "We hope y'all will come and visit us ag'in and recommen' the Mountain Ranch Hotel to yer friends."

The trip organizer said, "Mother Nature wanted to have something to brag about when she was creating these mountains. This area attracts outstanding people who do amazing things. We have enjoyed our visit more than we can put into words." All the guests gave Knox and the hotel staff a round of solid applause before they started toward their cars.

At the end of the week, Bennie and other staffers were surprised and elated as each got a shiny half-dollar as a bonus in their pay. She added all her coins to the money in her sewing box. Slowly she was gathering enough money to be able to return home after Kat finished the third grade. Her life was going exactly as she planned, and it was interesting too.

CHAPTER 11

FANNIE MAE

Time flew, and each day brought small surprises for Bennie and Katherine. Each of the surprises was a new learning experience as both discovered the vast differences in people.

One day, after they left the hotel and went into their room, Kat jumped facedown on the bed and began twisting her body and limbs in ecstasy while saying a long, soft "wheeeeeee."

"I'm having a happy spell," she said as her mother laughed. Kat asked permission to stay at school to play during recess because a new first-grader named Abigail had become her friend. "I'm going to have a happy spell, too," Bennie said as she told Kat she could stay at the school during recess.

Caleb Alexander, who always looked like he had just stepped out of a magazine picture, continued to come to the restaurant for meals. Bennie always approached his table with slight unease, expecting him to talk about his church services. But he mentioned the services only casually, ordered his food, ate, and left.

Bennie missed her friend Ellie almost as much as she missed her mother. She needed to have someone to talk with and began to consider Fannie Mae a good friend, as they talked about the many rumors and actual happenings in Helen. They worked together shelling peas and butter beans, breaking green beans, stripping tough stems from turnip greens and collards, and peeling potatoes. One of their subjects was the popular mountain rumor about a hidden fortune in gold left by the departing Indians. One version of the tale said it was hidden in a cave, and another version said it was buried in the ground between two well-marked trees. Still a third version talked about a strange mountain man who was guarding the treasure.

They both talked about how they could use the fortune, and each promised to tell the other if they found where the fortune was hidden. They laughed together, sardonically.

"I guess the treasure was found almost one hundred years ago when they found that gold nugget over near Duke's Creek and all those miners scrambled in here," Bennie said.

"Your Cousin Melvin musta found tha treasure. Tha's how he built that purty house," Fannie Mae said.

Bennie only laughed. She didn't admit that she had been amazed that her cousin had such a beautiful home.

She and Fannie Mae talked while they washed and dried all the pots, pans, and dishes. First the hotel operation and its staffers were their subjects, and then they talked briefly about their own family members. Bennie learned that Fannie Mae's husband had been a tenant farmer before they moved to Helen where he joined the group of black woods hicks. "His bro'hers wen' to Dee-troit. They 'as got more freedom ther', but we diden wanna make sech a long trip."

They were talking together when Bennie learned that religious worship wasn't the only venue shutting doors to a person who was simply trying to walk life's pathways.

Fannie Mae always refused to sit down and eat with Bennie although Bennie invited her many times. Fannie Mae finally explained, "Colored people can't sit down wi' white people. Ya know 'bout lynchin', don' ya? Colored people been hung jes fer talkin' ta white people."

"Surely, that's not true," Bennie said.

"Is gospel. My mama's daddy 'as white, an' my daddy wan' all his chilun to know not to cross the color line. A few year' ago, he make us look at a colored man get hung. We knew 'im well, 'n I diden look. They say he 'ttacked a white woman wi' intent to rape. Tha militia 'as called up to pertec' 'im whil' he 'as tried. They laughed 'n' told jokes 'bout 'im 'fore they hung 'im. Later, they sold pieces of tha rope that 'as 'roun' his neck, and my daddy bought me a piece o' tha rope and told me neber to fergit. Tha man's wife say he 'as wit' 'er an' it cou' neber of happen'."

Bennie couldn't respond.

"And we can't neber teche a white person, not eben to shake hands. I reckon it 'cause our colored skin might rub off on white skin," Fannie Mae said, with an ironic chuckle. "'Fore I came here, my bes' friend 'as white, bu' I neber sit down wid her to eat 'cause I diden wan' her to git in trouble. Colored people ain't s'ppose to be educated, bu' she learned me to read, and I'm teachin' my chilun."

Bennie suddenly realized that the Helen school had no black children. All the students were white. "I'm glad to have you for my friend," she said.

"Ya gotta be aware of the Jim Crow laws if you go outa Helen. Eben here, ya 'n' me can't be seen together. Ya know I al'ays come to work through the back doo' 'n' you come throu' the front doo'," Fannie Mae said.

"But that's because you live in back of the hotel, and I live in the front."

"No. It 'cause colored people cain go in a fron' door lessen it's their house."

"I heard about a white man here in Helen who got his colored friend out of jail," Bennie said. She wanted to say something good about a white person.

"Yeah, it's a brave white man who he'ps a colored man. Other white people 'bout killed that man 'cause he he'ped tha colored man."

The women talked about the South's rigid social system that imprisoned blacks and sometimes whites.

During their conversation, Fannie Mae said one thing that went deepest into Bennie's heart. Her dark face became deeply saddened as she said she was going to do everything she could to live a good life and give her children a good life. "But we can't neber hold a highfalutin job no matter how educated we is, 'cause air gran'dads and gran'mas were captured and brough' here in chains. Tha's hard ta fergit, and air faces show who we is. Air gran'paren's was treated lik' animals, and now we air jest tha same. We can't neber be proud."

Bennie didn't know how to respond, and after a minute she asked about the one thing that was frequently on her mind. "Do colored people go to church?"

"Oh, yeah. Colored people go to church alla time. We depen' on God to he'p us make it."

"Do you have a church here in Helen?"

"We'uns jes go to differen' homes. Sometimes we have the service under tha trees 'side the river. Tha's the bes' place."

"Do you ever say a person can't come to your church again?"

"We didn' 'xactly say that, but we told Jumpin' Joe Jimpson that he couldn' neber come to church ag'in when he 'as drunk. He 'as hollerin' 'n' no one could get him to shet up. We kudden eben hear tha preacher."

Bennie smiled and said, "I'm glad you didn't completely stop him from attending."

"Where do ya go to church?" Fannie Mae said.

"I went to hear the traveling preacher when he was here. I may go to church here someday," Bennie said.

CHAPTER 12

HE RETURNS

The weeks zipped by as Bennie learned about life and people. She wasn't accustomed to big holiday celebrations and didn't consider it necessary to prepare for Christmas. She became worried during the middle of December when Kat began wondering what Santa would bring her. She was able to knit her a blue hat and put it under her pillow.

Dorothy invited them both into her parlor on Christmas day and presented them with colorful wrapped gifts. "Santa had to leave this under our tree for you," she told Kat, and the excited little girl opened the gift to find a china doll with a beautiful face. Bennie reluctantly opened her gift, apologizing because she couldn't return the gesture, and found the Mark Twain book, *The Adventures of Tom Sawyer*. She silently vowed to have gifts and always be ready for Christmas in the future.

In August 1914, Bennie found it hard to believe that she had been in Helen a full year. One Sunday morning, she and Katherine were walking to the hotel to begin their day when Bennie noticed four young men walking away from her on Main Street. Each was carrying a small bag and had probably just got off the train. One of these men's red suspenders made a big X across his back, and she could tell that he had light brown hair. Her heart beat faster, and she watched them as long as they were visible.

"Who was that?" Kat said.

"I don't know, sugarplum. I was just trying to see where they were going," Bennie said.

The day's activities began and continued as usual, but Bennie could not keep her mind on her work. Her body was moving between the tables and kitchen as usual, but her mind was back on Tray Mountain. The man she saw that morning looked like the man she knew and loved when she was fourteen years old.

She remembered exactly how she first saw him that day long ago. The wild azalea bushes on each side of the cabin steps were covered in orange blossoms, and she was sitting on the steps, sewing. He walked toward the cabin, wearing a pale blue shirt with red suspenders. Black straps across his shoulders indicated a backpack. A beard covered his face, and his hair reached his shoulders.

She kept glancing toward him until he arrived at the cabin. "I'd like to speak to your daddy," he said.

"My daddy's sick," she answered.

"What about your mama?"

"I'll get her." Bennie rushed in the door, found her mother in the kitchen, and told her of the strange visitor.

When her mother came to the porch, the man said, "My name's Keats Anderson, and I hear you need some work done."

Her mother told him that she couldn't use him although a man was desperately needed for certain chores. When he said he would work for room and board, she asked him to wait and told Bennie to get him a drink of water.

Alone on the porch with the stranger, Bennie hurried to the well, filled the gourd dipper with water, and handed it to him. After a long drink, he handed the dipper back to her and sat down on the steps. She sat down on the edge of a rocker and leaned toward him in anticipation.

Finally she broke the silence, saying, "Where are you from?"

"Savannah," he said.

"I know that's far away and near the ocean," she said before becoming silent again.

Her mother returned to the porch and said she had talked to her husband and, together, they prayed for God's guidance. She told the young man he could come inside and bathe and stay for a week. After he was provided clean clothes owned by Bennie's father, he was offered her father's shaving razor and strop. Bennie was shocked when her mother said, "I also can cut your hair if you would like."

Later Bennie could hardly believe that he was the same person who had greeted her earlier. His brown eyes were shining, and Bennie couldn't look away. She had never seen such a handsome young man.

After eating a full meal, he walked around outside to plan his work and then slept on the settee. He began work the next day, carefully cutting down a giant oak tree with gnarled limbs that was leaning toward the cabin. On the following days, he patched the roof and used Glory, their mule, to plow the garden. His plowing allowed them to add corn, green beans, squash, and okra to the potatoes they had planted earlier.

Bennie talked with him as much as she could and learned that he had left college to come north. The same as hundreds of other people, he had come to northeast Georgia hoping to find gold.

His work was well done, and one week with the Sheldon family turned into two. He began to sometimes hold Bennie's hand when they were away from the cabin, and it seemed totally natural. The first time he kissed her and held her in his arms, it seemed that the world was hers. The following day, they were in the forest searching for sang when she joyously gave herself to him.

The next morning he had gone, leaving a brief letter to her on his pillow.

Dear Bennie,

I have been miserable all night because I don't know what to do with you. I'm afraid I have hurt you and pray not.

You are wonderful and will always be beautiful. You can have whatever you want and must live your life to the fullest. I fear that I will keep you from fulfilling your dreams.

I leave with great sadness,
Keats Anderson

Bennie couldn't believe he was gone and waited months for him to return. Later she vowed she would forget he ever existed. She destroyed the letter but knew the words still would be engraved in her mind.

When her baby girl, Katherine Keats Sheldon, was born, her sadness about his departure only deepened. She thought she was not worthy of him, and he had written the letter in kindness to her. She wished the stranger she saw that morning had not worn red suspenders. Whatever the reason for Keats Anderson leaving her more than six years ago, she definitely did not want to see him again.

"Young woman, would you please bring Coca-Colas for everyone at this table?" a guest said, snapping her out of her memories.

She would make sure her path did not cross the path of the red suspenders.

Caleb Alexander came in for supper and talked to her briefly about his new job in the sawmill office. "I think the sawmill company is being sold, but I'm not sure," he said. "I know that the work is continuing because new men are being hired."

Bennie told him that she heard some of the workers had left to join the army and expected to go to Austria. She was speaking of the Great War and had looked up Austria on the global map at the school. The war soon involved all the countries of Central Europe, later becoming known as World War I.

It was almost closing time for the restaurant when two men walked in. Bennie turned her back on the two as soon as she saw them. She didn't know what she was going to do because one of the men was Keats Anderson. *It's* him. *I wonder why he's here.*

Her thoughts were muddled as she tried to decide what to do. Finally she decided she would treat the men as if they both were total strangers. She turned around and approached them.

"Please come with me," she said, not looking at Anderson.

She led them to seats at the windows and said, "We have fried ham or fish, green beans, corn, vegetable soup, Coca-Colas, tea, and coffee. What can I serve you?" She was still not looking at Anderson although she knew he had been staring at her. She was able to take their orders for drinks and food, serve them, and take their payment without ever looking at Anderson.

She knew he was still staring, but he didn't speak to her.

She reopened the restaurant doors to let them out and cleaned their table without looking at him, knowing all the while that she would have to talk to him sooner or later.

Kat was sound asleep in the kitchen, and Bennie woke her to go to their house. Holding her hand, she left the hotel and saw the outline of a figure beside the walkway.

"Bennie, please stop and talk to me," Anderson said.

"Good evening," Bennie said. She kept walking, searching for a way to ignore him.

"When did you come here to Helen?"

"In August a year ago," she said.

"Did your parents come with you?"

"My parents are dead."

"I'm glad you're doing so well. Who is this little girl?"

"This is Katherine. She has to go to school in the morning. I've got to go." Bennie started walking toward their house again, and Anderson didn't move.

CHAPTER 13

THE FATHER

After she and Kat were in bed, Bennie couldn't go to sleep. She tried to think of ways to avoid all future contact with Keats Anderson. She couldn't go back home. She had found the courage to come to Helen so her daughter could go to school, and she was now about to enter the second grade. She must find the courage to stay in this town with Keats Anderson near.

She had to look at the good things about her new life. She had been in Helen more than a year, but only an hour in Helen was enough to know that it was an astounding place. She knew that some towns, like Philadelphia, were hundreds of years old, and Helen first began growing into a town only four years ago. Old towns had old buildings and old houses, but Helen was full of new buildings and new houses. Old towns were full of history, but Helen was full of excitement and new experiences.

Helen had a new hotel that was attracting caravans of rich tourists from Atlanta throughout each spring, summer, and autumn. Mr. Knox already had turned away visitors because all the rooms were filled.

She and Kat were no longer skin and bones, and she had money. She had met a lot of people at the restaurant, and she claimed some as friends. Kat was learning rapidly and had a good friend at school. Coming to Helen was the right thing to do. She wished she could talk to Mr. Williams again like she did before moving. She wished she could still talk to her friend Ellie Rigsby.

The next morning, Bennie was thankful that it was her Monday off, and she wouldn't have to work in the restaurant. She didn't take Kat to eat a good breakfast but gave her cookies and cider, then walked her to school.

She wanted to stay in her room because she didn't want to see Kat's father again. "Never trouble trouble till trouble troubles you," her mother had always said.

Bennie walked to the school to bring Kat back for lunch, and she continued writing in her journal that afternoon. She didn't leave the house except when she went back to the school to get Kat.

The next morning at breakfast, Caleb Alexander told her that he could come and escort her to the church service on Sunday morning. Bennie reminded him that she worked on Sunday. He chuckled and said he would keep asking until she said yes.

On Friday, she saw Keats Anderson again. He came in for supper late that day and said he had just come from the Moccasin Creek timber camp.

He waited again for her and Katherine to leave the restaurant, and because seeing him stirred the old heartbreak, she became angry.

"Please stay away from me. I don't want to talk to you," she said when he stepped toward her.

"What's wrong? I thought we were friends," he said.

"A friend doesn't hurt someone so much that she almost commits suicide," Bennie said, rapidly walking away from him.

Why did I say that? Why am I talking to him? Bennie didn't know if she was mad or scared.

"Please wait. If you don't talk to me today, I'll be waiting for you until you do."

Bennie stopped.

"Please tell me what you mean," Anderson said.

Bennie was silent a minute. Finally she said, "It was hard for me to understand why you left me."

"Just tell me who you married. Who is the father of your daughter?"

"I don't owe you an explanation. Please don't come near me again."

Bennie almost broke into a run, dragging Katherine with her, and Anderson called out, "I have something for you. Please wait."

She stopped again, and he walked up to her.

He said, "Just hold out your hand."

After a minute, Bennie held out one hand. Anderson dropped a silver thimble into her palm.

Bennie could hardly believe her eyes. "Where did you get this?" It was her mother's thimble, which had disappeared from the cabin's front porch more than a year earlier.

"I found it on the road to your cabin. I was surprised to find you gone and the home closed."

She turned to walk toward her door, saying over her shoulder, "Thank you for giving it to me." She walked in and shut the door behind her, leaving him standing in the road.

"Mama, who is that man? What does he want?" Katherine said.

"He's a man who once came to us on the mountain and helped Nana and Papa. That was almost seven years ago."

"He wanted us to stay and talk to him."

"He helped Nana and Papa, but he's not my friend."

"Why did he give you Nana's thimble?"

"Nana's thimble disappeared from the front porch when I was sewing there. Remember? I had to buy another one from Mr. Williams. He said he found it on the road to our house, and I think a crow must have stolen it. You know how they like shiny things."

Bennie knew her words about Keats Anderson not being her friend were hard for a little girl to understand, but she didn't know what else to say.

After Kat was in bed, she went out to sit on the front porch. Once again she went over the changes in her life. Back on the mountain, she had only her daughter, and now she was in a new mountain town. She once wondered if she could get a job, but she became a waitress in a popular hotel beside the biggest sawmill east of the Mississippi River.

As she was thinking, the sawmill's generators shut down and the town's lights went out signaling nine o'clock. She began thinking solely about Keats Anderson, her first fascination with him, her total enrapture, and her heartbreak on his departure. The sadness led her to more mournful thoughts.

After the church banned her and her baby, she thought she did not deserve to live. Keats Anderson had abandoned her, and after Katherine was born, the church pastor said she had to bring her baby's father to the church. When she couldn't do this, she was told that as an unmarried mother she was not fit to attend. No person other than her parents wanted her presence, and she decided she could not continue to live.

In desperation, she found a tree limb, tied a rope to it, and stepped on a small wooden stool with the rope knotted around her neck, intending to end her life. *I am worthless. My life is pointless*, she thought. As she was about to jump off the stool, a vivid image of her baby's face popped into her mind. Katherine didn't have a father, and if Bennie kicked the stool away, she wouldn't have a mother. Her life was extremely important to her baby girl.

Her own mother and extremely ill father would be completely heartbroken. *What gives me the right to rain misery on others because I am miserable? I must take care of my baby girl.*

After what seemed like a long time, Bennie removed the rope, stepped off the stool, and slowly took it and the rope back to the barn. Years later, she looked back on her decision to commit suicide as foolish, but she never forgot the hurt she suffered from being deserted by the person she expected to spend her life with and being judged unacceptable by her friends.

Bennie moved her chair to the edge of the porch and looked upward with the intention to send thoughts up to her mother. Looking into the dark heavens, she could see the Milky Way. Millions of stars blazed a path across the sky as if God had been planting stars in a measured pattern but suddenly threw out big handfuls with abandon because he had become too tired.

I'm tired too, and I can't seem to decide what I should do about Keats Anderson. I wish I could scatter all my thoughts away like the stars are thrown out in the Milky Way.

CHAPTER 14

NOT ANOTHER DADDY

Bennie planned to approach Anderson the following weekend when he was back in town. She would tell him she was married because that would make him stay away from her. If he asked her husband's name again, she'd say it was none of his business.

On Friday evening, a woods hick who frequently came to the restaurant destroyed her plans. "I hope I don't catch what tha' new man's got. He's hurtin' bad," he said.

"What happened?" Bennie asked.

"Tha' new Anderson man 'as brought back on a stretcher."

Bennie wanted to know what the problem was, but she couldn't ask questions.

The town's nurse solved her problem Saturday morning when she told Bennie that Keats Anderson wanted to see her. He was suffering from a fever and was unable to bend his neck. He had been diagnosed with spinal meningitis and was being isolated in a tent north of town to prevent spread of the disease.

Bennie stared silently at the nurse, who told her where the tent was located. "When I left him, he was speaking clearly, but he may be confused when you see him," she said. Bennie could only whisper, "Thank you."

She didn't know what to do. If he had spinal meningitis, he would die, and if he had asked for her, she must see him.

Later that morning, Bennie walked up the road to find the tent beside the river. She hesitated and didn't know what she should do when she heard groans. The flap opened, which was the tent's door, and the doctor walked out and saw her. Removing his face mask, he said, "I don't like to have this man here, but there is no other place to isolate him. I'm keeping this flap down because too much light for him is painful. We asked him if he wanted anything, and he said he wanted to talk to you. You can talk to him, but don't go in. I've given him thirty drops of laudanum, and he may begin hallucinating," he said.

She slowly walked up to the tent door, opened it slightly, and saw him on the cot inside. "Mr. Anderson. I understand you wanted to see me," she said.

After another groan, Anderson spoke in a low voice. "You don't like me, and you must forgive me. I didn't mean to hurt you."

Before Bennie could think about a response, she said, "I loved you, and you left me with a child."

Anderson responded with more groans. Finally he said, "What did you do?"

"I loved her and raised her. She's now been promoted to the second grade and does well in school."

"Is she the little girl who is always with you?"

"Yes, it's Katherine."

A long silence.

"I wish I had known. I would have loved her too."

All the hurts poured from Bennie without control. "I was banned from the church because I had given birth without being married. I lost all my friends. For a while, I didn't want to live."

More silence.

"I've been working on a ship out of Savannah that stays on the ocean for years. I came back because I want to marry you. I even had a wedding ring made for you," Anderson finally said.

Bennie didn't dare go into the tent.

After a long silence, she said, "If I marry you, Katherine will finally have a daddy. I'll go find someone now to help us if you're sure that's what you wish."

"Please find someone."

Bennie spent an hour hunting for Caleb Alexander, but no one could tell her where he was. At the Hayden home, Hubbard Hayden said he was licensed to perform wedding ceremonies. He would join her and Anderson early on Sunday morning.

Bennie went back to the restaurant to finish the day. Taking Katherine into their room that evening, she told her the plan. "We have to go see Keats Anderson tomorrow morning. I'm going to marry him, and you will have a daddy," she said.

"My daddy is dead. I don't want another daddy," Kat said.

"What do you mean? Why do you say your daddy is dead?" Bennie said.

"I remember Papa. He died a long time ago."

"No, honey. Papa wasn't your daddy. He was your grandfather. Keats Anderson is your daddy, and I was mad at him because he left us. Today he said he wants to take care of you."

Kat could not accept the idea that her mom was going to marry and give her a dad. Nothing Bennie said put her at ease.

On Sunday morning, Izzy came to work in the restaurant, and Bennie dressed herself and Katherine more carefully than usual. They left to meet Mr. Hayden at nine o'clock for the marriage ceremony. Walking toward the tent, they saw the doctor and another man carrying a stretcher.

"Ms. Sheldon, your friend has passed on," the doctor said. "He's not suffering anymore. Can you notify his family?"

Bennie answered, "No," although her mind had become blank.

"Some men are digging a grave for him up in Robertstown. We have to bury him today."

Hayden arrived and talked to the doctor. Bennie had not moved and still was silently staring when a wagon with Anderson's body began moving north. Katherine had not made a sound.

Bennie thanked Hayden for his condolences and said, "I must go to breakfast." Still holding Kat's hand, they went to the restaurant.

Bennie was saddened by Anderson's death, but she didn't grieve. She had deeply grieved for years about his departure, and she had not become accustomed to his presence again in her life. His death didn't end a valued friendship but simply closed an old heartbreak.

She and Katherine were finishing their meal when Hayden approached her. "Can you take the things Mr. Anderson had in his pocket?" he said. He offered her a money clip holding dollar bills and cigarette papers, some change, a small cloth bag holding tobacco, and a small silver ring. Bennie didn't want to take them, but Hayden said he couldn't give them to anyone else. She found a small paper bag, put them in it, and placed the bag in the trunk where she kept her money.

She was going to work Tuesday morning when the woods hick who had told her about Anderson being sick approached her. "I wonder what they did with Anderson's smokes an' tha' silver ring."

Bennie didn't want to answer and said, "I don't know."

"He showed me tha' ring, and it 'as real silver 'cause it 'as made from a fifty-cent piece. He said a friend made it for him when he was on the ship. It 'as smooth as silk. If I ever need a ring, I'm gonna find somebody who kin make one like it."

Bennie had slipped the ring on her finger before putting it away, and it was a little too large. *I'll keep his things unless someone from his family comes here. I can never wear the ring*, Bennie thought.

CHAPTER 15

HANK LOVES ME

Bennie's working hours prevented her from regularly seeing her cousins, although they lived in the same house. On a Monday evening early in November, before her second Thanksgiving in Helen, Bennie went around their house to knock on the front door. Dorothy opened the door to her. "Oh, mercy, you didn't have to come around to our front door. Come in. Come in," she said.

Melvin got up out of his chair, placed a book on the side table, and nodded his head to her. "I hope everything is okay," he said. He was a little alarmed at the unusual visit.

"We're fine. I just wanted to tell you about a stranger who was asking about you," Bennie said.

"Where did you see him? What did he look like?"

"He was at the hotel for supper last night. He was trying to sell possums he said he caught in a rabbit box, but Mr. Gale didn't buy them. When I took his order, he asked me if I knew a Melvin Rhodes. I told him yes, and he asked where he could find you. I told him I didn't know because I wanted to ask you if I should tell him," Bennie said.

"What did he look like?" Melvin asked again.

"He had dark hair and a long beard. He wore overalls, and his clothes weren't clean. He wore a dirty old felt hat, and he didn't even take it off in the restaurant."

"If someone wants to talk to me, they can come to my office," Melvin said. Dorothy insisted on serving them apple juice, and Melvin asked Bennie to look at his books and find one she wanted to read. Bennie borrowed *Riders of the Purple Sage* by Zane Grey and was fascinated later to read about a woman who was thrown out of her Mormon church because she wouldn't marry another Mormon.

Bennie was finding her life better than she had imagined. She was learning about all kinds of people, some she didn't want to know, when Katherine came home from school with an obvious problem. While inside the restaurant, she didn't speak at all, simply looking at her tablet but not writing. Bennie could hardly wait till quitting time when she could take Kat to their room. She wanted to find out why she was so quiet. She didn't have a temperature, but maybe she was getting sick.

Neither of them spoke as they walked toward their room. It was mid-November, and the weather was colder, with the nights sometimes harsh. Cousin Dorothy had given them two draft stoppers called snakes, round cotton tubes stuffed with dried beans, to put at the bottom of their outside door and the bottom of the window. She also had presented them with a braided rug that covered the floor on one side of their bed.

Once inside, Bennie put the snake at the bottom of the door to block the cold air. They removed their coats and shoes, keeping on their cotton socks. They quickly put on long-sleeved flannel gowns and heavy knit caps that covered their ears. Three quilts were on their bed, and as soon as they snuggled together under their covers, Bennie said, "Katherine, what's wrong?"

Her daughter didn't answer her and kept her head turned away.

"Sugar, please tell me what's wrong. Are you feeling bad?"

"I wish Hank didn't love me," Katherine said.

Bennie was surprised. "Hank? Are you talking about Hank Bristol? The boy who was at Mrs. Ross's house? Did he say he loves you?"

"He said he loves me, but I can't tell anyone."

"When did he say that?"

"Today. He took me in the bushes behind the school so no one could see us."

Bennie was silent for a minute. *I shouldn't have let her stay at school during recess.* "Tell me about it," she said.

Katherine kept her head turned away. "He took me in the bushes and said I had to take off my drawers. He said he had to kiss me all over my body because that's what his daddy does to his aunt, and his daddy loves his aunt."

Bennie stopped breathing.

I must be calm. I must take care of my baby. She felt the same emotions she had felt when the newborn Katherine was first placed in her arms. She told herself at that time that she would always do everything possible to make sure her baby had a good life.

"Where was the teacher?" Bennie said.

"On the playground." The teacher had wanted the children to play outside and use up excess energy.

"Where was your new friend, Abigail?"

"She was mad at me and playing with another girl."

Silence.

"Did you take off your drawers?"

"Hank said it was okay for me to take off my drawers because I'm a bastard. He pulled them down."

Bennie stopped breathing again as thoughts whirled in her head like the colors in a twirling kaleidoscope. Hank was in the fifth grade. She had never thought about something like this happening. *What words can I use to explain that Katherine must never allow such acts?*

She wanted to scream, but she made no sound. She pulled the quilts closer to Katherine.

Finally she told Kat to turn her head and look at her. She looked straight into her eyes and said slowly, "Sugar, you can't take off your drawers for any person. You can't take off your clothes anywhere except here in this room with me. Promise me you'll never take off your clothes for anyone."

When Bennie didn't say anything else, Kat finally said, "What is a bastard?"

The word was horrible, but it opened a small door for more words from Bennie. "The law says a bastard is someone who does not know who their father is or someone who cannot inherit his father's property." *I must be calm.* "We know who your father is. Remember? Your father was Keats Anderson. He left us for a long, long time. I'm just glad he gave you to me before he left."

Earlier Bennie had talked to Katherine about being churched, and now she was talking to Katherine about being called a bastard, but she still had not tied the stories together. She didn't know how she could explain to a child that her parents had not married. That was the reason she was banned from her church and the reason Katherine was called a bastard or woods colt. A child and an unmarried mother could suffer ostracism or banishment from society throughout their lives. Bennie knew no way to explain it to Katherine.

"You must promise me tonight that you will stay away from Hank. If he asks you to go with him away from the other children, you cannot go. Promise me you will never take your clothes off again for another person. Promise?"

Kat promised, and Bennie prayed aloud that her daughter would always remember. She later found sleep impossible. During the night she remembered that Kat had said Hank's father performed the same act on his aunt. *Hank's father is a terrible man. He condemned me for the same thing he's doing. He's making love to a woman without being married to her. How dare he have said his children can't play with Kat. I wish a tree would fall on Hank's father.*

Morning came, and Bennie hurried to the school during her morning break. She saw Kat outside with the other children playing "Who's got the thimble?" The teacher was standing in the schoolhouse door. Miss Tatum stepped inside the door, and Bennie tried to speak calmly as she reported Hank's act, but she couldn't keep her voice from rising.

The teacher acted as if she was being told about a lost shoe. She talked about how children always like to explore and how they mimicked adults before she finally said she would keep an eye on Hank and Katherine.

I must not be afraid. I must do whatever is necessary to take care of my little girl and let her go to school. Bennie kept reciting the words to herself. She did not know she was following an ancient Buddhist tradition of repeating words called a "mantra" to gain spiritual transformation. She only knew that fear would destroy her and that she must be strong for Katherine. She wished she could get her hands on Hank and shake him till his teeth rattled. No, Hank was a child. She wanted to confront Hank's father.

She could do neither. Either act would draw attention to her and Kat. She was thankful that Katherine was playing with other children and didn't see her mother visiting the school and talking with Miss Tatum.

CHAPTER 16

THE KILLER

On Thanksgiving morning, Bennie offered a special prayer, giving God thanks that she was still in Helen, for her job, for her collection of money, for allowing Katherine to go to school, and for Katherine's friend, Abigail. She went about her usual routine but would have gone back to her home on the mountain if she had known how her life was about to change.

Local hunters brought wild game to the restaurant, including turkeys. Herb said wild turkeys were too skinny and opted instead to offer roasted venison or fried chicken for Thanksgiving.

Bennie never ceased to be fascinated with his cooking, and the Thanksgiving menu included pear flambé. Ripe pears were peeled, sliced, seasoned, and fried in hot sugar before a small amount of applejack, a local brandy made from cider, was poured over them. Bennie used a match to set the pears on fire before she took the flaming dish to one of the tables.

Both schoolchildren and mill workers were on holiday, and Kat was mesmerized each time she watched her mother serve the pear flambé. Some of the woods hicks came to the hotel at noon for their Thanksgiving dinner. Still others came for supper.

Bennie's body was aching with fatigue when she and Kat headed for their room in the early darkness. A scream pierced the air and stopped them as they crossed the road. Bennie stood stone still. Katherine wrapped her arms tightly around her mother. The scream cut the air again. Children playing along the road stopped hollering and laughing. Helen became deadly quiet. The scream was coming from the side of their house. Telling Katherine to wait, Bennie crept to the edge of the house to look around as she heard loud sobs.

Cousin Dorothy was huddled over a figure on the ground, saying over and over, "Answer me, Mel. Please answer me, Mel." Bennie ran to her and then staggered backward. Cousin Melvin was lying facedown on the ground, and she could see a small hatchet handle protruding from the top of his head.

She hurried toward the road to go for help, and met Chief Alton Richardson, Helen's single law officer, and three other men running toward her. Bennie stepped aside as they ran past her.

Katherine was holding on to her mother again, and they slowly walked back to Cousin Dorothy, who now was surrounded by the men. Questions to Dorothy didn't get answers. Between sobs, she said only that she returned from the Haydens' home to find Melvin lying in the yard.

The hatchet, the size of a tomahawk, was deep in the top of Melvin's head, and a man put his hand on the handle, intending to move it, but it didn't budge. He changed his position to stand over his head with a foot on both sides, grabbed the handle with both hands, and pulled it away.

Finally one man pulled Dorothy aside while two other men spread a wool army blanket on the ground. They turned Melvin over onto the blanket, and, with one man at each end, carried him toward the hospital.

Bennie put her arm around Melvin's wife, but Cousin Dorothy wanted to be with her husband. She grabbed the edge of the blanket and walked beside him, still sobbing quietly. Bennie stood looking at the large stain of blood on the ground before she and Katherine also started toward the hospital.

It took the doctor only a short time to tell Dorothy that Melvin had been shot in the chest but had been able to get away. His attacker apparently chased him and slammed the sharp hatchet into the top of his head. The doctor wet a cloth and cleaned the blood from Melvin's forehead, closed his eyes, and placed a smooth, clean river pebble on each eyelid. He tied a cloth around the head and chin to keep the mouth closed. The face already had become different, unfamiliar, because it was lifeless. Melvin wasn't in it. Bennie was relieved when the doctor spread a sheet over the body.

Dorothy was no longer sobbing but was simply staring into space. She got up and went to the lavatory where she washed her bloody hands and wiped a spot of blood off her face. She returned to the seat, and Bennie was holding her hand when the Haydens came rushing in and put their arms around Dorothy. "How did this happen?" both said at the same time.

"I don't know," Dorothy said quietly.

The couple began telling Dorothy to come to their home and asked Bennie if she also would come.

"What can I do for you, Cousin Dorothy?" Bennie said.

"There's nothing anyone can do," she said.

Bennie waited a few seconds before saying she and Katherine would return to their room.

Neighbors were standing around the front of the Rhodes house and asking questions when they returned, but Bennie could tell them only that Melvin Rhodes had been killed. No one reported seeing unusual actions or hearing a shot or any other strange noise. Questions of who, how, and why filled the air, but no one had answers.

Bennie was afraid to enter the house. Neighbors asked her to come with them, and one man, Obie Nash, said he would search the home. He stepped inside his front door, got his shotgun, and walked into the front door of the Rhodes's home.

After he came out and said it was safe, his wife, Elizabeth, walked with Bennie and Katherine into their room. She put an arm around Bennie before saying, "We'll be listening if you need help."

After being sure all the doors were locked and preparing for bed, Bennie said a prayer longer than usual and got into bed. Almost immediately she heard a knock on the back door, and she let Dorothy and the Haydens into the other part of the house, but they soon left again. She locked the door, and Dorothy took the key with her.

Much later Bennie was still awake when she heard Cousin Dorothy's voice. She got up and walked into the parlor. Caleb Alexander was standing at the front door with Dorothy.

"We'll sit up with your husband tonight at the clinic," Caleb said, honoring the tradition of holding a wake and making sure the family was never left alone with a dead body. "You should rest. Your husband has already been welcomed into heaven, but we must have a nice service to honor his life. What day for the service would be best for you?"

"Day after tomorrow," Dorothy said. She didn't say the words aloud, but she desperately wanted to see and talk with her mother. She wanted to allow time to dig the grave, have the funeral, and then she would get on the train and go to Atlanta.

"I'll get everything ready," Caleb said, and he turned to Bennie. "Miz Sheldon, please send for me if I can help you," he said as he backed out and closed the door.

CHAPTER 17

COUSIN DOROTHY

Bennie walked with Cousin Dorothy into her bedroom. She told her she would check all the outside doors and leave her own room door open into the kitchen so Dorothy could more easily call out to her.

"How could this happen?" she asked.

"He had no enemies, and it wasn't a robbery. He must have been mistaken for someone else. The Haydens helped me take off his clothes and dress him in his black suit before rigor mortis set in. His wallet was still in his pocket."

The room filled with silence.

Finally Dorothy said, "Mel enjoyed life so much, and he loved living here in the mountains. He was always saying, 'Look at the mountains,' and talking about how he wanted to always live near these mountains. I wish I could find a casket with a window and not bury him. I want him to always see the mountains."

Bennie was almost loss for words. She said, "Cousin Melvin's soul can fly over the mountains. He can see them all now. We'll have to think about the service. Did Cousin Melvin have a favorite hymn?"

Dorothy named favorite hymns, speaking very slowly as if she was drained body and soul. "I think it would be proper to sing a Christmas song. It isn't long until Christmas now, and his favorite was 'Angels, We Have Heard on High.' I'd also like for us to sing 'Beneath the Cross of Jesus.' The last verse says, 'I ask no other sunshine than the sunshine of his face.'"

Bennie wrote down the names of the two hymns and hoped someone would know all the words. Dorothy declined her offer to stay in the bedroom with her before saying the sheriff wanted to talk to them both the next day.

"I'll wake Kat for school in the morning like I always do," Dorothy said, insisting that she would do it despite Bennie's protests.

After Dorothy was in bed, Bennie walked back into her room. She still couldn't believe what had happened. Cousin Melvin had always been her link to the rest of the world. She had not asked him for help since she came to Helen, but his near presence always made her feel safe. She didn't want to think about her future without having him nearby to ask for aid or guidance.

She was getting into bed again when she realized that earlier she had been standing in front of Caleb Alexander with her hair down and wearing only her long flannel gown. He already knew that she walked around town without an escort, and now he had seen her indecently dressed. Her thoughtless action probably had confirmed to him that she was like the bad women who lived in the Commercial Hotel.

The next morning, Bennie quietly left for work, going out the back door and down the steps. Duke was lying under the steps as usual, but he didn't get up and greet her. She stopped and called him, but he didn't move. When she walked around where she could see his head, she saw the wide cut. Dark dried blood was on top of his head and around his mouth. He was dead.

Neither she nor Katherine had missed his joyous welcome the evening before.

She felt numb. The person who killed Cousin Melvin must have hit their dog on the head with the hatchet. Why would someone kill a friendly dog? Duke already had made friends all over town, and nearby residents knew that he was Katherine's dog. Tears filled her eyes as she grabbed the feet of their faithful four-legged friend and dragged him to the side of the house. She put him under the bushes so Kat wouldn't see him. He could be buried later.

She had been shocked by Cousin Melvin's death but not hurt and saddened the way she was with the death of Duke. The dog was a loyal friend and a long-time member of her own family. He was always friendly with Helen residents, but he must have been suspicious of the person who killed Melvin. Duke's death indicated that the person was a stranger, not one of their local friends.

She was quiet at the restaurant, only responding briefly to questions. Later that morning, Sheriff Richardson asked to talk to Bennie. Herb told Bennie to take him to the second-floor sitting room for privacy.

Feeling like she was in a bad dream, Bennie told the sheriff about the man who was in the restaurant three days earlier and asked if she knew Melvin Rhodes. "He asked me where Cousin Melvin lived, but I didn't tell him. The man who killed Cousin Melvin also used that hatchet to kill my daughter's dog. There was no reason to kill our dog. Duke was friends with everyone, but I found him under our steps this morning," she said slowly.

Later Herb told her that the sheriff also had talked to him. He repeated again what he told her several days earlier. "I don' know for sure, but I think that man askin' for your cousin 'as from Dahlonega 'cause he was sellin' possums, and he said a rest'rant in Dahlonega always bought his possums."

A beautiful oak coffin—darkly stained, heavily varnished with a winged angel carved on the lid, and lined with well-padded white satin—was brought on the morning train for Cousin Melvin. A satin-bordered, see-through veil was included to drape across the open coffin during viewing and keep out flies. Bennie wondered about the cost of the coffin and thought of the unpainted pine coffins lined with unbleached muslin that Horace Rigsby and his sons made for both her father and her mother.

At midmorning, the body was moved to the Rhodes's parlor to await burial. The Haydens and two other couples took turns sitting with the body, and Bennie heard their low voices off and on through the night.

A grave for Cousin Melvin was dug in the small cemetery in Robertstown where Keats Anderson was buried, a place sometimes called North Helen. His funeral was conducted the next afternoon in the Rhodes's home, and Bennie left work to attend. The midday sun made it warm enough to go without coats, and she wore her white embroidered blouse, black skirt, and hand-me-down dress shoes from her mother. Katherine accompanied her in her blue percale, made from the skirt of her grandmother's dress.

Friends walked into the home, viewed the dead body in the coffin, and then flowed out the front door onto the porch and into the yard. Williams, the peddler, came in and told Bennie to contact him if he could help her. Williams, Dorothy, Bennie, Katherine, and the Haydens stayed inside the parlor.

Caleb Alexander, who had borrowed the Haydens' well-worn Baptist hymnal, stood just inside the front door to lead them in the hymns Dorothy selected. Here and there, people held tablet pages where Wylene Hayden had written the lyrics of the hymns, and people crowded around them to see all the words.

Wearing a black robe with a white collar, Alexander said Melvin Rhodes had gone to a place that was even more beautiful than the mountains around Helen. "He believed in Jesus, and Jesus said, 'In my father's house are many mansions: if it were not so, I would have told you. I go to prepare a place for you.'"

A horse-drawn wagon took Melvin's body to the Robertstown cemetery, but Bennie and Katherine went back into their room, changed clothes, and returned to the restaurant. She was concerned about Cousin Dorothy, but the Haydens were with her, and she didn't want to be away from work too long.

"I wish we could have had a funeral for Duke like the one for Cousin Melvin," Katherine said. The day before, neighbors helped Bennie dig a grave for him, and both she and Kat had cried as they talked about how he had always been their loyal friend. Using a small, sharp rock, Kat scratched "My Duke" on a large flat stone to cover his grave.

The next afternoon, Bennie was serving the first customers when Dorothy walked into the restaurant. She was dressed in black with a wide-brimmed, veiled hat and a street coat. She walked straight over to Bennie and said, "Can I talk to you a minute?"

Surprised, Bennie looked to see if the early customers were served before saying, "Come with me." She took Dorothy upstairs to the sitting room.

After they were seated, Dorothy reached into her coat pocket and pulled out a white envelope. "Here is the deed to our house. I'm going back to Atlanta, and I know Melvin would want you to have his home."

Bennie glanced at the envelope held toward her. "What do you mean?" she said.

"I went to Cleveland to see a lawyer today, and he made you the owner of the house. I'm never coming back to Helen, and I don't want to sell the house to strangers. You are Melvin's family, and now you own the home he was so proud of."

"I can't take your house. You can't do this," Bennie said, emphatically.

"You have to take the house. The deed now shows that you're the owner. I'm leaving," Dorothy said. She put the envelope in Bennie's lap, got up, and hurried toward the stairs.

Bennie ran after her, grabbed one of her arms, and tried to hold her. She couldn't let Dorothy leave her. She tried to thrust the envelope back into her hand, but Dorothy wouldn't take it. "You have to let me go. I want to go home," Dorothy said, on the verge of crying. Bennie didn't want to make a scene and watched helplessly as Dorothy hurried down the steps.

That evening, she went into the other part of the house to make sure all the outside doors were locked, and she and Katherine slept in their room as usual.

They snuggled together under the quilts for warmth. Bennie still thought about the angel watching over her, but she felt totally alone and vulnerable to unknown threats. *A vicious killer is here with us. Why did he kill Cousin Melvin?*

CHAPTER 18

THE BUGGY RIDE

The next day, Sunday, Bennie was helping Fannie Mae with the dishes from the noon meal when Mrs. Hayden, her gray hair showing at the edges of a fancy cap, came toward her, followed by Izzy. "We planned to take Dorothy for a ride this afternoon, but she's gone. We want you and Katherine to come with us. We have room in the buggy," Mrs. Hayden said.

Bennie said she had to work, but Izzy said she had come to wait on customers so Bennie could have the afternoon off.

Bennie hesitated, not knowing how to respond as Mrs. Hayden looked at her expectantly. Feeling as if she was caught in a web of outside forces, Bennie removed her apron and grabbed her bonnet and gloves. After putting on her coat, she helped Katherine put on her coat, and they followed Mrs. Hayden out of the restaurant.

A big double buggy with covered top and sides sat on the main road. Caleb Alexander and Mr. Hayden were sitting on the front seat, and Alexander had the reins of two well-matched young horses, black and glossy. When he saw Bennie and Mrs. Hayden approaching, he immediately twisted the reins around the dash rail and jumped out. He came around the buggy and offered each a hand to help them onto the backseat. Then he picked up Katherine and sat her beside her mother.

The buggy lurched forward as soon as he picked up the reins again. *I shouldn't be here. I should be working. We all should be looking for the person who killed Cousin Melvin*, Bennie thought.

Mr. Hayden turned to look at Bennie and said, "You need to see Nacoochee Valley. It's something to be proud of. I'm sure guests in the restaurant have been asking you questions."

Mrs. Hayden made general comments about the weather and its effect on their growing collards and turnip greens as the buggy rolled quickly south on the Unicoi Turnpike. They crossed the first bridge, and Bennie watched the passing scenery as she tried to get her thoughts together. They soon were at the granary, and Bennie saw a tall building across the road decorated with latticework. A sign on the front said Rooms for Rent.

After they slowed down behind a one-horse buggy also traveling south, the horses clattered across another bridge and began going around a curve. Bennie felt uneasy about the lively, prancing horses and her presence with the trio. Suddenly the thick roadside trees disappeared, the view opened, and Alexander stopped the buggy.

A large white house with a red roof towered above many white farm buildings. Bennie had never imagined anything like it. She was finally getting to see the farm called West End that she had heard people talk about.

Trees stood in front of the home, and neat round shrubbery lined a walkway to the front door. Behind the home, a man, probably a farm worker, was walking along a path from one building to a much larger two-story building. "That man's going to the dairy barn. This is the farm owned by Dr. Lamartine Hardman, and it's the most beautiful house here in the valley," Alexander said.

Bennie realized they were waiting for her to speak, and she said, "That's where the restaurant's milk comes from. It's a palace, isn't it?" She had been deeply impressed by the beautiful Mountain Ranch Hotel and the huge mill. But she had never seen anything before that looked like the Hardman house. "Rapunzel must have let her golden hair down from that tower for the prince to climb up," she said, referring to the well-known fairy tale. Mrs. Hayden chuckled.

Alexander said, "That house was built back in 1869, only four years after the war ended. Georgia was still under military rule and the so-called Reconstruction. The little room at the top allows someone to see a good distance and watch for approaching danger."

"What kind of danger?" Bennie said.

Her intense interest in his words enthused Alexander. "The war was followed by at least ten years of total chaos. The state was economically destroyed. Union soldiers were sent here to hold order, but they didn't know how. The slaves were freed, but didn't know how to take care of themselves. The farmers, who previously had owned slaves, needed farmhands but had no money to pay them. Small groups of armed and violent Confederate soldiers still roamed, and that's when the secret vigilante group called the Ku Klux Klan was formed," Alexander said.

"And the KKK helped us survive the Yankees and their Reconstruction," Hayden said.

"The KKK might have done good things, but I always think of its murders and white supremacist lectures," Alexander said with frustration in his voice.

He continued after a few seconds. "These Georgia mountains didn't see much of the disorder, and this farm was built by Captain James Nichols, a former Confederate colonel from middle Georgia. The tower could be there for protection, or it could only fulfill the home's Italianate design, which requires such a room on top. I think it's called a belvedere," he said.

All four were enjoying the view—the rows of arched windows, the red roof, and the wide eaves adorned with artfully shaped supports.

Alexander started the buggy forward again and stopped in front of the house. At the right of the road was a green pasture filled with brown Jersey milk cows. In the center of the pasture was a large mound of dirt with a white red-roofed gazebo on top flaunting intricate lacy woodwork that matched the house. Blue mountains provided a background for the scene.

"That's an Indian holy place," Mr. Hayden said, looking toward the mound.

"I'll go ask if we can walk out to it," Alexander said, pointing to a small wire gate. He jumped out and ran to the front of the Hardman house. After he knocked on the door, Bennie and the Haydens watched as a man came out and shook Alexander's hand.

They talked much longer than expected, and on returning to the buggy, Alexander apologized and said he had asked him several questions.

"Do you know Dr. Hardman?" Hayden said.

"Yes, he's the one who invited me to come to Helen," Alexander said. He held a hand up to help Bennie to the ground, and Katherine jumped down beside her.

The Haydens walked arm-in-arm toward the gate, and Alexander pulled Bennie's hand inside his arm. Bennie was holding Katherine's hand, but she was totally aware of the man beside her. She wanted to pull her hand off his arm but didn't want to be rude.

"Just imagine what this valley was like when it was filled with the Cherokees. Think of Indian houses all over this pasture, women cooking over small fires, and children playing here and there," Alexander said.

"The Cherokees were forced to leave their homes, and thinking about them makes me sad," Bennie said.

"It's appropriate that their march to Oklahoma almost one hundred years ago is called the Trail of Tears. Have you read any of William Bartram's writings? He was traveling up in Rabun County back in 1776, more than one hundred years before they were removed, and he described the Cherokees as agreeable, hospitable, and happy people. Their intelligence has never been disputed, and their departure is a shameful part of Georgia's history," Alexander said. "But white people and Indians feared each other, fought and killed down through the years, and Indians were in the minority. I guess they would have been forced out even if gold hadn't been found on their land."

Bennie discovered her love of history when she was a child at the Nacoochee Institute. She had never known a person who knew so much history about the Georgia mountains. She wanted him to continue talking. "Why is this mound a holy place?" she said.

"It used to be much bigger, and Cherokees had a council house on top. They kept a fire constantly burning in the council house and sometimes did ceremonial dances there. The dancers would run down the side of the mound and bathe in the cool river. I don't think anyone's ever dug into this mound, but it's believed that it's where Indians buried their dead."

The Haydens had stopped at the foot of the mound. Mr. Hayden started up the mound, but Mrs. Hayden stood still. "It's a holy place, and I don't want to walk on it," she said.

Behind her, Alexander said, "The gazebo is called a summer house and was built as a place for entertainment. But she's right. We can show our respect for the Indians by not walking on the mound."

After a minute, they all returned to the buggy, and Alexander continued driving east, pointing out an ornate little church that was as lovely as the big farm building. "That's the Nacoochee Presbyterian Church that was built by the Confederate captain," Alexander said. They passed a large white building on the left, which had been an Indian trading post, and a couple of workers on the right who were bundling brown stalks of corn.

Bennie stopped looking at the passing scenery and looked at Alexander's light brown hair curling around his neck and ears and his strong hands on the reins. She had to admit to herself that he was a handsome man.

He drove about two miles farther to a small store that also was the Nacoochee Post Office. He jumped down and went inside to purchase sugar cookies for all.

Back in the buggy, Alexander turned it around to return to Helen when a rabbit ran under it and flew between the two horses' legs. The buggy lurched forward so fast that it bounced slightly, leaving barking hounds behind it.

Bennie grabbed Kat with one hand and the seat with the other, her bonnet falling backward. She held on for dear life as the horses sped back toward their stables with bits in their teeth. Alexander was standing up and leaning back on the reins. Hayden had grabbed both the dash rail and seat and was shouting, "Hold 'em. Hold 'em." Mrs. Hayden also was clutching young Katherine as well as her seat and saying, "Oh my. Oh my."

The horses were back at the Hardman farm before Alexander was able to slow them. They still were dancing forward with small scampering steps as they trotted over the bridge and back toward Helen. Bennie continued to clutch both Kat and the seat.

Alexander stopped at the Rhodes home but turned sideways in his seat instead of getting off the buggy. "I guess everyone has heard that the sawmill is about to be sold. That's what Dr. Hardman was asking me about," he said, looking at Hayden.

"Yes, I've heard rumors, but I didn't know if it was true. I wonder what will happen to the mill," Hayden said.

Alexander stepped off the buggy, walked around the back, and held his hand up to Bennie. "I'm sorry if you were scared. These young horses belong to a friend of mine," he said.

Bennie's bonnet had swung around and was hanging under her chin. Her hairpins were gone, and she brushed hair out of her face before she took his hand. "I've never traveled like that before," she said.

He laughed. "I'm sorry it happened. I'll give you a ride in a motorcar next time."

Bennie didn't respond but helped Kat down and turned back to the buggy and the Haydens. "Thank you for giving me something else to think about," she said, with a slightly trembling smile.

"You must come to church services at our house," Mr. Hayden said.

"Maybe I can someday," Bennie answered. She thanked them again, pulling her bonnet back over her head, grabbing Kat by the hand, and walking toward their room.

Bennie went back to the restaurant in time to tell Fannie Mae about the trip before she had to serve the supper guests. That night she wrote in her tablet, *I should have thought of a way to decline the invitation today. I hope I don't have to be with the Haydens and Mr. Alexander again.*

CHAPTER 19

THE RENTER

Bennie wrote to Dorothy at the Atlanta address, asking her to please come back to Helen. She missed Dorothy's presence much more than she missed Cousin Melvin. She had not realized before how much Dorothy meant to her, and now she missed her constant kindness. She still had not received a reply, but it had been only a week since Cousin Dorothy left.

Christmas was coming, and remembering her failure to prepare the previous year, Bennie wanted this one to be extra special. Planning a new project would help get her mind off her worries, and questions about Cousin Melvin's killer as well as Cousin Dorothy's absence never left her thoughts.

To help her plan a gift for Katherine, Fannie Mae brought her two-year-old "wish book"—the Sears, Roebuck & Company catalog—to the restaurant, and Bennie used her work breaks for two days to look through its more than seven hundred pages.

The thing that Katherine needed most was a new pair of shoes. During cold weather, she still wore Bennie's old moccasins with new deerskin on the bottom. The second evening she tore a blank page from her journal and asked Kat to stand first on one foot, then the other, while she carefully drew a line around each foot.

"Are you going to draw a picture of feet?" Katherine said, giggling.

"I'm going to send this page to Santa Claus and ask him to bring you a new pair of shoes for Christmas. Do you like that idea?"

"Oh, please ask him for shoes like Abigail wears. They're black, have a thick bottom with a heel, and they button up over her ankle," Kat said, her eyes shining.

Bennie found a picture in the catalog that matched Kat's description, and she ordered oxblood-colored shoes with two pairs of matching hose and sent the drawing of Kat's feet to Sears and Roebuck. She included more than one week's pay in the envelope to pay for the shoes and the postage for mailing them back to her.

She had not imagined that she would be able to order new shoes for Kat and it would be so simple. She couldn't stop thinking about a man she learned about as a child. It was long before Helen was created, and the man traveled from over the mountain all the way to Gainesville to get a pair of shoes for his young child. He drew around the child's foot on a piece of paper and took it with him. The trip to Gainesville and back took an entire week, and when he returned with the shoes, his young child was dead from the croup. *Life in the mountains now is so much easier*, she thought.

Later Bennie began wishing she had enough space in their room to put up a Christmas tree. Neighbors on each side of Cousin Melvin's house had offered their assistance over and over since his death. Now she wanted to invite them in for wassail and cookies to repay them for their kindness.

At the restaurant, Herb Gale said he heard that Dorothy deeded the Rhodes property to her. "We're still living in our room. We're keeping the house ready for Cousin Dorothy when she returns."

The next day Mr. Knox summoned her to his office. "I understand you have a room you can rent to my brother's wife," he said.

Bennie hesitated before she said, "No, I don't have a room." *Nothing is a secret in this town.*

"Herb said ya own the Rhodes home now. 'Ave you rented the room that ya were livin' in?" Knox said. "My brother's supervisin' one of the mill's biggest lumber camps, and 'is wife needs a room so she'll be here for his weeken's. I hope you'll rent yore room to 'er."

Why on earth can't he put her in one of his hotel rooms? I know they're not all filled now, Bennie thought as she walked back into the restaurant.

"I guess it'll be better to have another adult in the house until the sheriff finds Cousin Melvin's killer," Bennie told Fannie Mae.

She decided she could not rent her cousins' bedroom to someone who might not take care of it, so she replaced the sheets on the bed she and Katherine used and prepared it for another person.

The next day Bennie met Rosalee Knox, a tall, bosomy woman wearing high-heeled shoes and a silky brown fur coat. The hemlines of her dress and coat stopped well above her ankles. Bennie had no way of knowing that this woman would become an encouraging friend.

Izzy was helping with supper guests, and Bennie picked up one of her new renter's two bags and escorted her to the room. "I'm sorry this room is so small. Rooms in the hotel would give you more space," she said.

"Oh, I can't stay at the hotel. Ab would be very upset. He's always been jealous of his brother," Rosalee said.

The new renter was a talker.

"Well, call me if you need something," Bennie said.

"How much is this room gonna cost me?" Rosalee said.

"My goodness. I didn't think about that."

"What do people pay for a room at the hotel?"

"They pay two dollars a night, but they have bathrooms with inside toilets, and that price includes their meals," Bennie said.

"Well, I'll pay you one dollar a night if you'll let me use your bathroom," Rosalee said. She also had money and was a woman of quick decisions. Bennie was surprised because she and Kat had always used the wash bucket and chamber pot in their room.

"That can be arranged, and one dollar a night will be okay," Bennie said. "I must go back to work."

Rosalee took off her fur hat, which matched her coat, and revealed a complete view of her hair. It was cut just below the ears and arranged in a soft, fluffy style with straight bangs across her forehead.

Bennie waited for her to take off the coat. "You can put your hat and coat on this nail," she said.

"Yes, I have good wooden hangars in one of these suitcases," Rosalee said.

She took off her coat, and Bennie looked at her silk dress and long pearl necklace. It was hard to stop looking at her.

The next evening, when she and Katherine returned to the house, Rosalee came into the kitchen and told her she was looking forward to being with her husband during the weekends.

"Where's your husband?" she asked Bennie.

"Katherine's father left us before she was born, and now he's dead," Bennie said.

"Well, I hope you divorced him," Rosalee said. She was emphatic with all her words, and this sentence revealed real annoyance.

Bennie had heard the divorce procedure described as bad and sinful. The preacher in her church said more than once, "What God hath joined together, let no man put asunder."

She couldn't tell Rosalee that she had never married Katherine's father, so she attempted to change the subject. "What do you plan to do for Christmas?" she said.

"Oh, Ab and I will go to Gainesville for the holidays. My church there has a good Christmas program, and Mom will be cooking a big dinner. What are you going to do?"

"I've been thinking of putting up a Christmas tree and inviting the neighbors in for tea and cookies."

"That's a perfect way for you and your daughter to celebrate Christmas. Preparing for that will help you forget all problems."

CHAPTER 20

CHRISTMAS

Rosalee's words seemed to free Bennie's mind of hesitation. She didn't know any way she could find Cousin Melvin's killer, and she was doing all she could to contact Cousin Dorothy.

She immediately began thinking about Christmas decorations. The next day, one of Herb's friends found her a beautiful cedar tree, perfectly round, about four feet high, and ideal for the parlor. Bennie told Kat that she would have to create decorations.

Kat cut her used tablet pages into slim rectangular pieces. Fannie Mae gave her a large wrinkled beet that still had red juices. She sliced it and rubbed the wet side on the paper. Then, using the white of a fresh egg as glue, she joined circles of paper and made them into a dark red chain that could reach twice around the tree.

Everyone in the restaurant kitchen became involved in the decorations. Izzy, who had softened her attitude, brought in popcorn to string, and Fannie Mae brought a small corn-shuck doll she had made for the angel. Before she went home for Christmas, Rosalee took one of her gold pins, which was shaped like a star, and fastened it to the head of the corn-shuck doll before it was placed on top of the tree.

One week before Christmas, Bennie got her package from Sears and was shocked to also have a letter from the White County Court of Ordinary. The letter said she owed seven dollars and seventy-five cents in property taxes.

What does this mean? Why did they send this to me? How did they get my name?

Rosalee saw the letter on the kitchen table and said, "That's more than a week of what I pay you."

Bennie knew she would have to take money out of her little box and take it to the White County official. She would be keeping the house safe for Dorothy, and after all, she had never paid rent to her cousins. Paying the property tax for them would be repaying their kindness.

On her day off from work, Bennie wished she could go to Melvin's grave, but she remembered what he said about her walking alone. She wrote words to him on a page from her journal, saying, "Cousin Melvin, I wish you could tell us who attacked you. We miss you, and I'm keeping your house safe for Cousin Dorothy." After signing it, she threw it into the fire, letting the smoke take her words into the sky.

Christmas was three days away when Bennie went to the neighbors' houses and invited them to come for wassail and cookies on the holiday eve. On that day, the hotel restaurant was going to close at six o'clock in the evening and stay closed on Christmas Day. She already had invited Herb, Izzy, and Fannie Mae, telling them to bring their families. Each readily agreed to come, but Fannie Mae said she couldn't attend. Bennie didn't know the right words to make her change her mind.

The pleasure expressed by the other invitees increased Bennie's enthusiasm. She didn't worry so much about using her cousins' home and could hardly wait to welcome people to her Christmas gathering. She hesitated about inviting Mrs. Ross because she was afraid she might bring Hank and Goldie Bristol with her. After deciding she had no reason to be rude to the Indian woman, she invited her. On the day before the event, Bennie walked up the hill during her morning break to invite the Haydens, and she also invited the family of Kat's new friend, Abigail.

She used the hot stove in the restaurant to cook apple cider with cloves, cinnamon, allspice berries, and brown sugar. She was changing into her white blouse and dark skirt when her excited daughter presented two holly twigs with clusters of red berries and said, "Herb gave these to me, and they're for you and me to pin on our dresses."

Bennie remembered her childhood when her own mother invited people into their home, and she fought off homesickness.

Guests soon filled the parlor and kitchen, and Mrs. Ross walked over with the neighbors. Bennie served the warm wassail in Dorothy's beautiful china cups and held her breath that none would be broken. She also baked sugar cookies in the restaurant kitchen, and now they were on four plates, two in the parlor and two in the kitchen.

The Clarks came in with their children, including Abigail. When they introduced their little girl, she said, "I'm pweased to meet you." Kat's friend was tongue-tied and especially small in stature.

Bennie was talking with her neighbor, Elizabeth Nash, when Mr. Hayden pounded his fist on the table, and said, "I want everyone to join us, and we'll go wassailing." Before getting a response, he said. "I'm sure everyone knows the words to 'Silent Night,' 'Hark, the Herald Angels Sing,' and 'Oh, Little Town of Bethlehem.'"

"How about 'Away in a Manger'?" someone said.

Obie Nash ran back to his house for his guitar, and thirteen people, including Bennie and Kat, walked across the road to the houses on the hill. Mr. Hayden didn't hesitate to lead them while Mr. Nash accompanied them, and they sang the first verses of two songs at each house. People came to their doors during the first song, and the carolers were always asked to sing another. Sometimes people put on wraps, left their houses, and joined the carolers. Apparently none of the homes they visited belonged to Jules Bristol because Bennie didn't see Hank or Goldie.

They had reached the last house on the hill when Bennie approached Mr. Hayden. "Can we go to the colored section of town?" she said.

"Do you know someone there?" he said.

"Yes, a woman named Fannie Mae works with me at the restaurant. Her husband's a woods hick, and they have three children."

For the first time, Bennie realized that she had never heard Fannie Mae's last name.

"Well, we can go there. It's not far, and we'll see if someone can tell us where she lives," Hayden said.

The group started down the hill toward "colored town," which was behind the small tannin factory on the west side of Helen. A man in the group said, "Where are we goin'?"

"I hope we can sing carols to Fannie Mae and her family. She works with me at the restaurant," Bennie said.

"Oh, I know where that family lives," the man answered.

Soon the group was at the home pointed out by the man, and they began singing "Hark, the Herald Angels Sing." It took longer for a person to open the door, but a child's face immediately appeared at the window. Soon Fannie Mae, a man, and three children walked out the door.

When the singing stopped, the man who had led them to the house called out, "Merry Christmas, Stretch."

Bennie said, "Merry Christmas, Fannie Mae."

The two on the front porch burst into laughter and applause. The carolers joined the laughter and thanked them for the applause. Fannie Mae ran back into the house and got a plate of cookies to offer the singers.

Hayden said, "It's getting late, and we must go to my house. I think Caleb Alexander is there waiting for us, and we can have a short worship service before we all go home."

Soon the entire group was crowded in the Hayden parlor, and Alexander was commending them for their caroling. Bennie didn't object to attending. It would be a short service, and she didn't want to call attention to herself.

Alexander looked over the group and said, "All we need to do is thank God for his son and for our lives here in Helen. Who wants to pray first?"

A number of people prayed aloud, one after the other, and after a period of silence with no one speaking, Alexander offered his own brief prayer. He then said people could return for another service at the Hayden home on Christmas afternoon.

Gunshots celebrating Christmas were sounding across the night when the carolers began filing out the Haydens' front door. Bennie was going out when Alexander touched her arm. "I want you and your daughter to come to our afternoon service tomorrow. I'll come and get you and then escort you back," he said.

Others were looking toward them, and Bennie didn't know how to refuse the offer. "What time is the service?" she said.

"We'll meet here at four o'clock," he said.

Bennie hardly spoke as she walked back to her house, accompanied by her neighbors. At her home, she wrote the whole experience in her journal and ended with *I must think of a way to avoid Mr. Alexander. He makes me feel confused.*

CHAPTER 21

A DAMAGED SOUL

On Christmas morning, Bennie could hardly wait for Kat to see what Santa had brought her. She was in the kitchen cleaning and thinking Kat was asleep when she heard her say loudly, "Mama, come look. I can't believe it."

She put the new oxblood hose and shoes on her feet. Bennie had to fight tears as she watched her little girl. Her excitement would not have happened if they had stayed on Tray Mountain.

After the shoes were fastened, Kat began walking around the room, holding up her gown to look at her shoes and then looking over at her mother. "Santa has never brought me anything like this before. They fit my feet too."

A half hour passed before Kat remembered that she had made a Christmas gift for her mother. She got her tablet, opened it, carefully tore out the back page, and handed it to her. It was a pencil drawing of Bennie in the restaurant. People were sitting at every table in the picture, and Bennie was carrying a pear flambé.

"Honey, I can't believe you did this," Bennie said.

"It took me a long time."

"Well, I want to keep it forever." The wonder of the day made Bennie think she might be in a beautiful dream. Magical delight was filling her life, moving aside the dark cloud of an unknown killer.

Leftover beans and corn bread brought from the restaurant the day before provided their noon meal.

Kat said she wanted to visit Abigail, and since Bennie had met Abby and her family, she walked Kat to their house. It was impossible to determine who was the most excited about the visit after Mrs. Clark opened their door and invited them in. Abby began showing Kat her new matching mittens and hat at the same time Kat held up her foot to exhibit her shoe and matching hose. *I'm glad Kat is Abby's friend*, Bennie thought.

After talking for a little while, Bennie said they had to return home. Mrs. Clark said, "Leave Katherine with us. We're goin' to the worship service at four o'clock. You kin get 'er then." Kat wanted to stay, so Bennie walked home alone.

She was reading another of the Rhodes's Zane Grey books shortly after three o'clock when a knock came on the door. Caleb Alexander was waiting outside, and she said, "It's early, and I'm not ready. Please go ahead, and I'll be there at four."

Caleb said, "Please come out here on the porch with me. I want to talk to you."

Bennie braced herself for the negative words she thought were coming. She stepped out on the porch and asked him to sit in one of the rockers while she sat down in the other and looked at him.

"You're always beautiful. You don't have to do anything to get ready for our service. You can come just like you are," Caleb said.

Bennie thanked him and waited for him to say that other people didn't want her there.

"I want to get to know you. I want to escort you to the service. Will you go with me?"

Bennie continued to look at him. When he learned what kind of woman she was, he wouldn't want to escort her anywhere. He was being kind now, but she wanted it to end.

"You don't know about me," she said.

"I know that you are very smart, honest, and a good mother to your daughter," he said. His eyes seemed to become a brighter blue.

Bennie knew she had to stop him. She could feel her body grow hot and knew she was blushing. "You should know that Katherine is a woods child and I was banned from Standing Oak Church after she was born. You don't want me in your church."

Caleb stared at her. Finally he said, "Churches have banned women and babies for centuries. It's wrong, and you must remember that Jesus said, 'Suffer little children to come unto me.' Can you let me escort you to the service this afternoon?"

Bennie heard what he said, but she could not accept it. "Please understand what I just said. A church said that I am a damaged soul, unworthy of Christian fellowship. My daughter hasn't even been baptized." Bennie wasn't so adamant anymore. She was pleading, and her eyes were filled with tears.

"I can explain my reasoning on this custom when we have more time. Now I can only tell you that preventing a mother and her child from participating in Bible study is not God's wish. The church that I organize will not do such a thing. Please answer my question. It's almost time to go to the Christmas service."

Bennie stared at him, trying to think. "You must understand. You will put yourself in trouble being seen with me. It will hurt your efforts to organize a church."

"Why don't you let me worry about that?" he said.

"I don't ever want to be told again that my presence is harmful in worshipping God. You don't know what the other people at the Haydens' house will say. I cannot come with you," she said.

He asked about Katherine and learned that she was with the Clarks. "Don't you want your child to learn about God?" he said.

Bennie stared at him silently. She had constantly talked to Katherine about God and felt insulted by the question. Finally she said, "I'll walk with you to the Clarks' house and get Katherine."

They both were silent as they walked to the Clarks. While Bennie was inside the house getting Kat, Caleb walked the short distance to the Haydens' home. The parlor was full, and Hayden was passing out sheets of paper containing the words of hymns. He was leading everyone in "O Come all Ye Faithful" when Bennie and Katherine slipped in.

Bennie looked around for the Bristol children as she always did, but they were not there.

Caleb began his message with the words "This morning, our children received gifts from Santa Claus. We received gifts from each other, and we were gladdened. Now we are here to thank our heavenly father for the gift of all gifts, his son, given to the world to forgive each one of us of our failures. Some of us here today have jobs that make a lot of money, others not so much money. Some can read and write with the best; others cannot read or write at all. Some are old; others are young. It does not matter who we are or what prevents us from proclaiming an earthly success. If we love God's son and try to follow the path he set for us, we all will have the same value when we stand before God in heaven."

Bennie was expecting words about bad people facing hell and damnation. She was surprised and felt an unexpected soothing of her thoughts. It was as if an invisible hand had brushed all negative feelings from her mind. The man who was saying these words said he was a preacher. Maybe this preacher would not condemn her. Maybe Katherine could be baptized.

When the service was over, Bennie took Katherine by the hand and waited on the porch for Caleb. She wanted to ask him if he could baptize Kat. As he came out, his face brightened on seeing her. He apologized for making her wait.

"People always want to talk to the preacher after a message, and these conversations are an important part of the service," he said.

They started walking toward Bennie's house. "How did you become a preacher?" she said.

"I was studying law at Emory College and rooming with a student who was studying theology. Law is a fascinating subject, but his remarks about the Bible helped me see that its words are intellectually challenging and emotionally rewarding. I want my life to benefit others, so I dropped the study of law and entered theology."

"Can you baptize my daughter?"

"I'll be happy to baptize your daughter. I hope you can bring her to more of our worship services."

That evening, after dressing for bed, she took up her journal and wrote, "When I came to this town, I was angry about a church, but I knew exactly what I wanted from life—a job, food, shelter, and school for Kat. Tonight I am no longer angry. Kat is finally going to be baptized, and I will teach her all I know about God and Jesus, but I no longer know exactly what I want from life."

CHAPTER 22

THE TRAIN

Winter passed without incident, except for one person who began to make Bennie nervous. She thought she had seen him before, and maybe he had been in the restaurant earlier. He was a middle-aged man with nothing outstanding or unusual in his appearance. He first asked to take her to church in Nacoochee Valley. After she declined more than once, she saw him following her toward the house. After noticing him behind her, she turned around and went back to the restaurant. After she could see him no more, she hurried home.

She saw him following her twice and asked Caleb Alexander what she should do. He immediately talked to Helen's one law officer. The officer began coming to the restaurant each evening and walking Bennie and Kat to their house. Eventually the strange man completely disappeared.

Summer came again with the restaurant offering blackberry and blueberry desserts. Suddenly Rosalee, who rented the room from Bennie, announced that she was going back to Gainesville to give birth. She had brought a bright change to Bennie and Katherine, and they wished she would stay.

Katherine was promoted to the third grade when Bennie faced another challenge. As she was drying dishes one morning, Fannie Mae said, "You tol' me you had a frien' named Ellie, didn't you?"

"Yes, why are you asking?"

"I think she in jail."

"Oh, Fannie Mae. I don't think so. That could not be."

"Sheriff say she kill' her husban'."

"Ellie has a house full of children. She would never hurt anyone. She can't be in jail."

"She got one of the chil'ren with her."

Bennie told Fannie Mae that she was glad she'd told her but that the woman in jail couldn't possibly be her lifelong friend. If only she knew someone to ask. "I'll go to Cleveland Monday and see if it's really her," she said.

Bennie had been away from her home and not seen or heard from Ellie for more than two years. Now she thought of her constantly as she prepared to go to Cleveland. She didn't want to ask anyone to drive her and decided that she and Kat would take the train. She had been hoping to take a train ride, and this was a good reason. They would take something to eat, stay all day, and return on the train. It didn't matter that Ellie would not be there, because they could walk around and visit the stores.

Although they had heard and seen the passenger train every day since coming to Helen, it was their first real visit to the Nacoochee Train Depot located across the river. On Monday, she and Katherine dressed in their best, carefully ironed dresses with hats and gloves, preparing to ride the train with great expectation and anxiety. Bennie was not anxious about unknown dangers but was afraid that her ignorance of proper procedures would make her look foolish. However, she never thought of backing out after she made a decision. She had done the same thing when she came to Helen. Now she was simply checking on a rumor about her old friend.

At the depot, she watched another person buying a ticket and followed him out to stand beside the track.

Although she had heard sounds of the train daily in Helen, she had never been so close. The ear-splitting whistle drowned out the loud hisses of steam, chug-chuga-chug of the engine, and clanging of the bell. All the loud noises, except the hisses, ended when the engine stopped, and the fireman swung out of the cab enough for her to notice his red earplugs.

The Monday train consisted of only the black engine, with its bright gold lettering that spelled Gainesville and Northwestern; a passenger car with some of its windows down; and the red caboose. Freight probably would come on later weekdays. Bennie was glad to recognize the face of the conductor/engineer as well as the fireman. She had seen them both in the restaurant and felt like she knew their work because of overheard comments. She knew the fireman kept busy adding sticks of wood to the fire and making sure water was added to the steam engine at specified stops. She knew the conductor saw some of the same people always taking the train.

Seven-year-old Katherine was excited and wanted to explore the colorful caboose, but the conductor placed wooden yellow steps at the entrance to the passenger car and motioned for all to climb aboard.

Other people got in the car with Bennie and Katherine. Two men were smoking and found a seat beside a can of sand. One woman carried a tin spit can for her tobacco snuff. All found seats and either looked out a window or whispered quietly to a seatmate. The passengers were quieter than worshippers in a church before preaching began. Katherine wanted to sit in the aisle seat but then changed with her mother to sit by the open window. After another exchange to the aisle seat, she noticed a passenger with a strange appearance. His face evidently was eaten by disease. The center of his face where his nose had once been was a large, open, raw sore. His eyes focused on nothing and showed no emotion whatsoever. He was two rows back, facing the back of Bennie and the face of Katherine, who was on her knees holding the seat back. Her eyes didn't move from his face, and he didn't try to hide but looked straight ahead.

Bennie didn't know what had consumed her daughter's attention but was pleased that she was so quiet and still.

"How will I know when we get to Cleveland?" Bennie asked the conductor when he took their tickets.

"I'll be sure you know," he said and smiled.

The train moved slowly, and she looked out the window. A passenger flagged the train to stop in Yonah, but it didn't stop in

Mount Yonah or Asbestos. After the conductor walked through the car announcing Cleveland, Bennie grabbed Katherine's hand to depart. She never saw the diseased passenger, but she immediately saw a tall man with a silver star on his shirt beside the train depot. As soon as he stopped talking to another man, Bennie asked him where the jail was located.

She added, "Do you have a woman there named Ellie Rigsby?"

"Sure do," he said, "and her little girl too."

Bennie only thanked him. *How could this happen? Thank goodness I'm here.*

CHAPTER 23

ELLIE

Cleveland's new depot, rebuilt after the previous one burned, was in the middle of town across the street from the large, impressive courthouse built of handmade blood-hued brick, and the jail was only a block away. Katherine told her mother about the man on the train as they walked to the jail, but Bennie couldn't listen and respond. At another time, she would have said, "Anyone suffering like this is usually kept at home. We should remember him in our prayers." The conductor could have told her that the man was returning from a conjurer on the mountains north of Helen, hoping her magic would cure his disease the same way rumor said warts were removed.

Bennie entered the jail, a two-story block building, and saw a man sitting just inside the door. He answered her question, "Yeah, she's in the first cell upstairs."

Bennie started upstairs, heard the soft giggle of a child, and unconsciously held her breath.

When she saw Ellie, she felt as if she were suddenly back on Tray Mountain. But, horror of horrors, Ellie was in jail. A toddler with a head full of blond curls was leaning out between the iron bars to see who had come up the stairs.

Ellie looked much older than she remembered. Bennie slowly walked to the bars and said, "What happened?"

Ellie's face crumbled and tears began. "I missed you so much. I thought I 'as gonna get a better life same as you," she said.

They both walked to the corner of the cell farthest from the men in other cells. In whispers, Bennie heard Ellie's story. In the cell across the narrow hall, a man was reading the Bible to his brother, and both had come to the Rigsbys' home asking for information about the Sheldons. "They 'as lookin' for yore cousin, Melvin Rhodes," Ellie said. "They said you 'as livin' a good life."

The men had visited Ellie Rigsby day after day, maybe camping out in the woods nearby. The older of the two men, Jim, who was slightly older than Ellie, eventually told her that he loved her. His much younger brother, Badeye, was severely retarded and depended on Jim for everything, Ellie said. He had lost his right eye to a ricocheting bullet when he was a child. He was catatonic, frequently stared into space for hours, and almost never spoke. She knew no name other than Badeye, the name his brother used.

Ellie's husband had a job at one of the lumber camps and came home only on the weekends. That's when he rewarded himself with whiskey. Jim decided that he didn't want the husband to be there at all and asked Badeye to shoot him. Badeye always did anything Jim asked.

"I 'as goin' to marry Jim 'n' come to live in Helen. I thought we'ud be friends ag'in," Ellie said.

The brothers were charged with murder, and Ellie was charged with conspiracy to murder. A jury of twelve white men pondered the guilt of the brothers for about three hours and returned a guilty verdict. Another jury of twelve white men considered Ellie's guilt for only half an hour, found her guilty, but recommended mercy. Jim and Badeye were sentenced to be hung, and Ellie was sentenced to life imprisonment.

Ellie's middle children, ages six, eight, and ten, were living with her husband's sister, while the oldest two, fifteen and nineteen, were working at a lumber camp, and the youngest was there in the jail.

"What happened to Wayne?" Bennie asked, referring to Ellie's invalid son who would be about seventeen and was totally dependent on his mother.

"Wayne died. He didn't suffer. He just didn't wake up. He was a perfect new baby and bright. One night, when he was eight months old, he cried too much, and his dad shook him real hard. He stopped moving and just never walked and talked," Ellie said. Bennie had never before heard the reason for Wayne's problems.

Saddened by this information, Bennie recalled that the little girl was once a baby in a shoebox behind the stove. Now the baby was named Angel and was walking and talking in jail. *I should take her with me. Surely I can find a way to care for her*, she thought.

Bennie stayed at the jail with Ellie and Angel until it was time to catch the train. They shared their midday food with Ellie. Bennie was glad she brought three of the big buttered biscuits from the restaurant. The sheriff's wife cooked for the prisoners and provided only two meals, one early in the morning and one in late afternoon. As she was leaving, Bennie gave little Angel a nickel and promised Ellie she would be back the next Monday.

Back at the restaurant, she told Fannie Mae everything. Herb heard some of the talking and told Bennie that Mrs. Ross, the half-breed woman, was available again for childcare. Bennie learned that Hank and Goldie Bristol's father, Jules, had remarried and moved his family away, and she visited Mrs. Ross, who readily agreed to watch after Angel Rigsby each day.

On Tuesday, Bennie asked Caleb Alexander if she could talk to him later. He said he would drop by her house during her afternoon break. After he knocked on her door, she stepped outside to her porch and asked him to sit in the other chair.

"I'm thinking about getting another child to look after, and I need a man of God to say a prayer for me," she told him.

Answering Alexander's questions, she told about little Angel wandering around in the White County jail.

"I'll be glad to ask God's blessings on you. You'll be okay. He already has blessed you in caring for your daughter, and he will bless you again," he said. "You must get that little girl."

After he left, Bennie felt relief and was confident that she would be able to care for Angel. *I wonder why that man's approval is important to me*, she thought.

On her next visit to the jail, Bennie explained her plans to Ellie and promised to take care of Angel as if she were her own child. Ellie reluctantly agreed. She had no choice.

Angel was not with her mother but was visiting a woman in the back cell. Ellie explained that the little girl had used the nickel from Bennie to buy licorice sticks. "I didn' know she'd go downstairs and out the door, but she found somebody sellin' candy. I didn' want it, and she give it to the woman in the back cell. She don't have no teeth, and she like licorice. She here fer sellin' her man's whiskey."

Bennie walked toward the back cell to get Angel, and Jim, the man who had been sentenced to death with his brother, called out to her. "Miz Sheldon, didn' you ever ask how yore cousin got that fancy house?" Bennie stopped and looked at him in surprise. He was the man who had been in Helen, asking more than once to take her to church and later following her outside the restaurant. "Melvin Rhodes stol' the gold I found 'n' saved all my life. If I'da got it back, we wudden be here."

Bennie didn't answer him but went on to the back cell to get Angel. He must have been the dirty, unkempt man who had asked where he could find her cousin. Walking past him again, she asked, "You killed Cousin Melvin, didn't you?"

"I ain't gonna talk to you no more," Jim answered.

Bennie considered his words a positive answer. He found someone who would tell where Cousin Melvin lived. He killed Cousin Melvin, and now he was sentenced to hang for killing Ellie's husband. She didn't say anything else. *I can't worry about something I can't change.*

She promised Ellie she would write to her and keep her informed about Angel. They wouldn't be able to visit because Ellie was about to be transferred to a woman's prison in Milledgeville many miles away.

Ellie got a flour sack with Angel's clothes off the foot of the jail cot. She hugged the baby, and her voice broke several times.

"You made me so happy when you were born. You will always be my Angel-girl. I'm leavin' you now, and you must always be good." Tears streamed down her cheeks as she and Bennie promised letters to each other. Bennie and Katherine carried the little girl to the train depot and returned to Helen.

Angel didn't cry as she left her mother but cried herself to sleep that night. She was placed between Bennie and Katherine in bed, and both patted her while rubbing her back, wishing they knew words to ease her aching heart. Their hearts were hurting too. She didn't cry when Bennie left her with Mrs. Ross but only sat quietly as if she were too scared to protest. She cried herself to sleep each night that week. When another child the same age began joining her at Mrs. Ross's each day, she finally began to relax and became more active at home with Bennie and Katherine.

Two weeks passed as Bennie anxiously awaited a letter from Ellie, giving an address for writing reports about Angel. A light rain was falling when she finally received a handwritten letter from a minister in Milledgeville.

Dear Ms. Sheldon,

Mrs. Rigsby had your name and address in her belongings, and I regret to tell you that Mrs. Rigsby is dead. She was put in a room with other women beside the kitchen. On the first day she was to work in the kitchen, she stabbed herself with a knife. The doctor could not save her."

May God grant you peace,
Herbert Goodin, chaplain
Milledgeville Prison

CHAPTER 24

CALEB

Only a week later, Caleb Alexander surprised people at his church by announcing that he was returning to Atlanta. Bennie was disappointed by the news. She considered him a valuable friend and didn't want to know she could no longer see and talk to him. She sent word that she needed to talk to him before he departed.

He was in the restaurant early the next morning. "I need to talk to you, and you said you need to talk to me. When can I see you?" he said.

"When are you leaving?" Bennie said.

"I'll have a service at the Haydens' this weekend, and then I have to leave." Caleb's blue eyes were pale, maybe tired, but definitely not as bright as always.

"I wanted to find out when you can baptize Katherine."

"She can take part in the baptismal service this weekend. I have three other children to baptize. But I still need to talk to you. Can you meet me at your house during your afternoon break?"

Without hesitating, Bennie answered, "Yes."

"What time will you be there?"

"At two thirty."

Bennie couldn't admit to herself that another chance to see him pleased her. Preachers chastised people, and he probably wanted to reprimand her about something before he left the area. Despite her trepidation, she began to count the minutes until the restaurant's clock hands reached two thirty.

He was standing on the front porch of the house when she reached it. She had taken her apron off before she left the restaurant, and she removed her bonnet, looking at him expectantly.

"Bennie, I first want to fully explain my belief in God. I'll make it as short as I can. Will you hear it?"

"God's angel always helps me," Bennie said, explaining what her mother had told her when she was a toddler. The simple idea had helped her stay positive and successful through many of life's challenges. "I know his son Jesus died for our sins, and I've been baptized. But yes, I'd like to hear you. Please sit down."

Alexander kept standing. "My belief in God has made my life a pleasure. Some of my friends in school argued that there is no God. If you're right, I asked them, what is the point of mankind and this wonderful universe? Of course, they had no answer.

"Since the beginning of recorded time, a few humans were searching for a way to make all people peaceful, respectful, considerate of others, and kind. The Bible says that more than a thousand years before Jesus was born, the children of Israel were given the Ten Commandments, prohibiting such things as murder, dishonesty, and cursing. People continuously looked for someone worthy to teach the qualities listed in the commandments, and they finally found that person in Jesus Christ, a wonderful, courageous teacher and fearless rebel man who talked about love. He was a powerful man, a carpenter, who chose fishermen as his best friends. We have stories about him helping a prostitute and a tax collector, so we know he helped all kinds of people. I have looked at other religions and their prophets. None compare to Jesus. One day I decided that I believed in Jesus, and a special peace came over me. The more I learned about Jesus, the more I loved him. He asked that people who believed in him spread his word to others. That's what I'm attempting to do.

"The King James Bible is a fountain of wisdom. It was put together by men who constantly prayed for God's guidance. The books of Matthew, Mark, Luke, and John were written by men who deeply loved Jesus. They reported happenings concerning Jesus that are almost identical to happenings in our society today. They didn't report Jesus ever making unforgiving judgments of a person who erred.

"The Old Testament contains a collection of short books written over fifteen hundred years before Christ's birth about traditions at different times in history. Some of the books, such as Psalms and Proverbs, are full of wisdom. The words in some of the Old Testament books reflect the communities from which they came, and now they are interpreted by men in today's communities. Unfortunately, men sometimes forget they are supposed to be guided by Jesus's continuous love and his Sermon on the Mount. Church leaders have always feared women and babies without a man to provide for them, and your former church feared that you would set an example for other young women, telling them that fatherless children were okay. It's sad, but that's why you were not allowed to attend the church without your daughter's father. Some members of that church would say it was because of fornication or sexual intercourse without marriage, but not having a man for support is the rock-bottom reason.

"I don't know how you became a mother, but I have observed you distantly for more than two years. You constantly demonstrate a proper life for your daughter and now the new little girl you've taken in. I know that you're a good mother and a good woman." Caleb stopped speaking, and both were silent.

Finally he spoke again. "I want you to become my wife."

Bennie could not have been more surprised. Her heart was pounding in her ears, and she simply stared at his face. He had not moved, had turned his face away, and still was standing stiff and straight a few feet from her. She didn't know what to say.

He looked at her again and said, "You don't have to answer me today, but I hope you will say yes. I will leave on the Sunday train, and I must visit my parents in Pennsylvania. I'll return and be in Atlanta for one year. I want to finish my studies, and I plan to come back here and build a church."

Bennie still didn't speak. She had almost stopped breathing.

"I admire you for your courage and determination in caring for your daughter. Now you are caring for another little girl. I admire you because you are walking a straight path in life despite the difficulty a woman has in supporting herself."

Silence.

"Will you say something?"

Finally Bennie almost whispered, "I don't know what to say."

"Just tell me if you will wait for me. I will write letters to you while I'm in Atlanta, and I hope you will write letters to me."

"I'll write," Bennie said softly.

"Good. We can exchange our thoughts about the future in letters. Maybe that will be easier." As he went down the steps, he said, "I'll see you Sunday."

Bennie went back to the restaurant, but a warm vision of Caleb and his words filled her head. *If his parents were in Pennsylvania, he must be a Yankee. But how could he be a Yankee? I've always been told that Yankees are bad, but he is so nice. My own relative was a thief, the man who killed him was from these mountains, and a Yankee has been constantly willing to help me. I definitely needed to learn that people can't be dropped in groups and labeled. Now what should I do?*

Sunday came, and Katherine was excited about being baptized. Bennie tried to ignore the fact that she was excited because she was going to see Caleb again.

At the service, Caleb assured the parishioners that he would stay in touch and return. At the baptismal service, he talked to the children who were about Katherine's age or older. After explaining the importance of the moment, he began, calling each by name.

"Katherine Sheldon, do you love Jesus Christ and want to follow the word of God?"

Katherine's yes was barely audible.

"I am going to use a drop of water on your forehead to signify baptism. We cannot immerse you in the river because it is too cold, and God does not like for us to make his children sick. Please know that this water immerses you into a totally new life as a child of God."

Katherine beamed at her mother, and Bennie smiled. She remembered being immersed in an icy stream for her own baptism, and red blood gushed from her nose over the new white dress her mother had made.

After the service, she waited to speak to Caleb. "You have taken a load of worry off my shoulders today. I can't tell you how thankful I am."

He took her hand and held it as his blue eyes, now bright again, looked into her brown ones. "The only thing you need to do is promise to write to me," he said.

"I promise," she said softly.

I understand what Mama meant when she said, "You need to learn people." Every person is different, and there is no way to know what another person will do. I must always know what I will do. I have to be sure I have decided what my hopes are.

Bennie was taking her first step along the scary pathway called love, or total personal commitment to another individual.

KATHERINE

CHAPTER 1

1932

Katherine stepped off the streetcar and stood under a small shelter before opening her umbrella and walking through the gently pouring rain toward Alabama Street. She felt extremely lucky because she had a job. She wanted to become independent and self-sufficient. She wanted to blend in with local people and avoid being labeled a yokel or hick. Despite her desire to befriend, she could never force a faked laugh at one of the bad jokes about hillbillies.

It was 1932, and Katherine lived in the bustling city of Atlanta, which was on the cutting edge of economic change. The city was exciting, but Georgia was one of the nation's poorest states. It still depended on farming's cash crops, and white farmers had an average cash income of only eighty-three dollars a year. Black farmers struggled to grow enough food for their families.

The state had two completely separate, side-by-side worlds, one white and one black. The only established contact between the two worlds occurred when black citizens did menial work for well-to-do white families. The white world knew very little of importance about the black world. Well-mannered, thoughtful white people referred to black citizens as "colored." Others used humiliating, hateful words. Whites and even blacks belittled any black person fortunate enough to get a few years of schooling. They were called *uppity*, a word designed to "keep them in their place."

The stock market crash three years earlier had brought the hard times of the nation's Great Depression. Atlanta churches ran soup kitchens, and one of the city's auditoriums was used as a sleeping place for two hundred men, white only. Outside the city, destitute families walking the roads and begging for food were a common sight, but they had no reason to drift through Helen, the mountain town where Katherine grew up.

The town's giant sawmill had closed with the steam whistle blowing for half an hour. Blowing that long was considered a proper but sad farewell, and it was necessary to remove steam from the sawdust-fired boilers for the last time. The train was gone and so were many of the families.

Georgia's farmers barely noticed the Great Depression because they were already suffering severe losses, most recently when the evil boll weevil destroyed the cotton crops. The Great Depression was more of the same. The new industrial age was said to produce a better quality of life, and Atlanta was moving into manufacturing, but rural Georgia wasn't changing.

Most farm families still were living exactly as their grandparents had lived. Homes, sometimes with as many as four rooms, were small, gray, and weathered. They were at least one foot above the ground with the corners on rock pillars and no skirting. Animals passed easily underneath to take advantage of the shelter. Chickens and sometimes a hog lived underneath, while a dog or two occupied the front porch.

Travel was by wagon or on foot, and water was hand-drawn from wells, while oil lamps provided any light after dark. If farmers didn't grow what they ate, they did without.

Prisoners, fastened to each other with heavy iron chains at their ankles—chain gangs—did the only maintenance on Georgia's roads, which turned into deep mud after a good rain. The Georgia General Assembly took its first step in building roads in 1923 when it added three cents a gallon to the price of gasoline, but in a democracy, projects paid by taxes were slow, slow, slow.

Railroads were still the main form of transportation, and they created Atlanta with fifteen rail lines flowing through the city. Georgia's few towns served by trains were more advanced.

Katherine's father preached at a small church in Helen and also taught in the free public school for white children. It was the only school in town, and law prevented black children from attending. Katherine or one of her parents frequently slipped into the colored neighborhood to a black friend's house in the evening to help her children and their friends learn.

Her mother loved to sew, especially after Kat's father bought her a Singer sewing machine. She could rapidly stitch strong seams by sitting in front of the machine and rocking a treadle at the floor, guiding cloth through the needle and bobbin. She was pleased when her sewing contributed to the family's income because preachers made very little money. If someone provided the cloth, pattern, and thread, she sewed the item for them and charged a small fee. She could use the "magic machine" to create an intricate dress, turning uncut cloth into a wearable outfit in one day if the buyer was available for fittings.

Politicians talked about living in hard times, and Eugene Talmadge, Georgia's commissioner of agriculture who was running for governor, said dirt farmers had only three friends: "God Almighty, Sears and Roebuck, and Gene Talmadge." He was referring to the white farmers. He promised that schooling would never be provided to black children. The blacks said that God was their only friend.

Talmadge called city residents "bums" and "chiselers." He wasn't against farmers getting relief, but if city dwellers were seeking relief, he said, "They should be lined up against a wall and given a dose of castor oil."

Women had gained the right to vote ten years earlier, but Katherine never listened to talk about a candidate for public office because she thought the words didn't apply to her. Now she knew about Eugene Talmadge because he hurt her family's black friend when he vowed to never let black people attend school. Casting a vote against Talmadge was something she could do to make her parents proud and support their black friends. Registering to vote was frequently on her mind, but she didn't know how to go about it.

CHAPTER 2

A JOB

Arriving under the shelter at Rich's back entry, she shook water off her umbrella, walked in, and took the elevator to the mezzanine, a fancy word for the large balcony between the first and second floors.

Before she came to Atlanta, she heard people in Helen praising Rich's with words of wonder. Now she was working in the amazing store. She replaced a worker who left to take care of her ailing husband, and she wondered what kind of new dresses would be ready for display that morning.

In a room provided for employees, she opened the small cabinet assigned to her and deposited her umbrella, wide-brimmed felt hat, handbag, and galoshes that covered her new beige shoes. She delighted in the shoes' new color, which was advertised as "pastel parchment." In the restroom, she glanced in the mirror to make sure every curl was still in place.

Katherine knew her appearance was important to success and knew her father had asked an old friend in Rich's management to give her the job. Before coming to Atlanta, she worked in the popular restaurant and hotel in Helen and saved every penny. Now she used the money for her attire, following examples of the women pictured in *Vogue* magazine.

Her plucked eyebrows were now in thin arches. Chamomile rinses after shampoos lightened the color of her newly shortened, pastel parchment hair. Sleeping every night with her hair in pin curls allowed her to sweep it across her forehead each morning into deep waves around her ears like Greta Garbo in *The Kiss*. She used "glow" makeup on her face, darkened her upper eyelashes with mascara, shaded her brown eyes with a touch of matching shadow, and used bright red color to make her full lips rosebud shaped.

The manager of the women's ready-to-wear department always wanted his clerks to look like women in high-fashion magazines, and Katherine enjoyed the challenge. Standing five feet seven inches, and weighing 125 pounds, she easily found dresses that were exact fits. She watched for the latest styles, and one more Rich's purchase would give her four store-bought dresses.

Clothes that she and her mother had made still were in Katherine's room. Some of their sewing materials came from colorful chicken feed sacks of smooth cotton. Matching sacks were bought from a woman farmer for twenty-five cents each, and two sacks easily made an adult-size dress, with scraps left over for a quilt. But she never wore a handmade dress to work. If a customer asked Katherine where she got the dress she was wearing, she wanted to answer "Rich's." To say it was handmade was unacceptable if she wanted to sell the store's clothes.

"Good morning, Mr. Jones," Katherine said as she entered women's wear. She never used his first name even though he had twice asked her for a date. Two other women's wear clerks arrived and spoke softly to her before they began arranging the new dresses on the walls and racks. Katherine quietly examined the other two women, making sure her own attire and makeup looked good in comparison, and they did the same with her. All three were slim, trim, and fashion-model perfect. One clerk moved a mannequin to a dressing room so its clothing could be replaced without exposing its nudity.

Katherine rarely joined the other clerks in general conversation because they were much older and always talked about husbands and children. She had neither and sometimes felt like an imposter in the world of women because she was not planning to marry and have a family.

NEW BEGINNINGS

All three clerks and Jones snapped to attention when the bell sounded throughout the eight-story building announcing that the doors were opening to the public.

Shoppers slowly began to arrive and wander through the displays. One of the first shoppers selected four dresses that she wanted to try, and Katherine ushered her into one of the little dressing room stalls with a tall mirror on the wall. "I'll wait out here. Please call if you need me," she said. She leaned against the heavily padded arm of a plush chair in the dressing room waiting area.

As Katherine waited for the woman to try on the dresses, she thought of her situation as a single woman without even the promise of a future husband and children. But she once had a husband.

Her mind wandered to what she called her "missing years." She met Julius Allen two years after she graduated from Rabun Gap School. She was sad and homesick when she first went away to school. She couldn't return home until the school year ended because Rabun Gap was almost fifty miles from Helen, and the roads were rough and dangerous. She became friends with several of the male students at school but never gave one a lifetime commitment. After graduation she considered herself fortunate to have a high school education and hoped she could find an educated husband.

Julius had graduated from high school three years earlier after eleven years of classes in Gainesville and enjoyed talking about the books he read. (It was about twenty years before Georgia public schools expanded to twelve grades.) She married him when she was nineteen years old only to discover along with him that he was very ill.

He worked in the woods for the Helen sawmill, but she never called him a woods hick, the slang term for such laborers. She sometimes called him Juke, but when he was in the sanatorium where others could hear, she always called him Mr. Allen.

Julius Allen was a tall, thin man with a pale, refined, clean-shaven face that women always noticed. Katherine was surprised when he became a regular visitor at her parents' home. He attended her father's church services, and on Saturday evenings he escorted Katherine to the weekly square dance at the Mountain Ranch Hotel. She had known him for almost six months when he proposed marriage and she accepted.

His parents rode the Gainesville & Northwestern Railroad to Helen to attend their marriage ceremony. Caleb Alexander, Katherine's father, performed the wedding in their local church, and it was completely filled with friends. The bride wore a white, floor-length, tulle dress her mother copied from a drawing in a *Harper's Bazaar* magazine, and she carried a bouquet of white roses. Her veil of fine tulle was fastened to her head with wild white honeysuckles. She had been too nervous to think about her appearance when the wedding was taking place, but her friends said she looked like a princess.

Little Angel, her fourteen-year-old sister, was the maid of honor, her only attendant. She wore a pale pink dress that matched her bouquet of wild pink honeysuckles. City dwellers called the lovely flowers "wild azaleas," but the mountain people called them honeysuckles.

Katherine's two young brothers, John, eleven, and Joe, twelve, served as ushers and completely surprised the bride because they escorted guests like professionals. Katherine didn't know their father had made them practice for an hour the day before the wedding. They were dressed identically in black suits made by their mom, white shirts, black bowties, and small boutonnieres of the beautiful white honeysuckles on each left lapel.

The newlyweds took the train to Gainesville, spent Saturday night at the DeSoto Hotel, and returned to Helen on Sunday. Julius wanted to return to work Monday because he was saving money to buy a house.

On their second weekend as husband and wife, Julius arranged a surprising experience. His parents had presented them with a rare bottle of champagne when they were at the DeSoto Hotel, and Julius said they must save it for something very special.

That Sunday morning they got up well before daylight and drove a borrowed buggy to Tray Mountain. After leaving the buggy, they each used a lighted lantern to find their way in the total darkness.

They climbed almost straight up, zigzagging between the trees and finally reaching the rocks on the mountaintop. They sat side by side, and he put his arm around her as the first gold streaks of sunlight reached across the sky. The gentle blue mountains seemed to be rolling away from them as far as they could see. Julius already had the champagne in two cups, and they toasted the mountains, the splendor of the sunrise, and their future together. Holding the world in their hands, they expected a future without limits. Katherine now felt like this memory belonged to another woman. A couple of times she depended on her memory to draw a picture of their view that morning, but soon she stopped drawing anything.

Julius continued his work at a distant lumber camp that week and returned to Helen Friday night on the logging train. Katherine was excited to see him and expected to attend the weekly dance at the Mountain Ranch Hotel, but on that third weekend he said he was chilled and needed to rest.

Katherine and Julius occupied the small room in her parents' house, and Katherine's mother was afraid Julius had consumption. Katherine knew fever was contagious, and she had to stay well to take care of him. She began sleeping on a cot separate from her husband and was careful to bathe him and often wash her hands with soap and water. She washed his dishes well, and after he didn't improve, she changed his clothing and bedclothes weekly.

Washing his sheets, handkerchiefs, shirt, and drawers was difficult and time consuming because she built a fire under the iron washpot and made sure the water became boiling hot. She added strong lye soap and stirred the pot's contents with a long stick. A tub of water from the river was used for rinsing, and everything was hung in the sun to dry.

Julius ate little and was losing weight. Sometimes Katherine and her parents thought he had changed for the better, but then the fever raged again.

After months of care, Julius showed no improvement, and the Helen doctor told them that a TB sanatorium was available not too far away. He advised that Julius enter the Alto Tuberculosis Sanatorium in Banks County, a trip that took an entire day if traveling by wagon and a half day by motorcar— that is, a half day if not delayed by one or two sudden flat tires. Katherine loved to drive the family's two-year-old Ford Motel T sedan and knew how to patch an inner tube to repair flats, but her father wouldn't let her drive to Banks County because she might become stranded on the roadside. Her father took Julius to the sanatorium, and he took Katherine to visit him once a month.

The sanatorium had been created about ten years earlier to isolate TB patients and give them proper nutrition and plenty of fresh air, while stressing proper sanitation to them and their families. Doctors had no medicine to fight the dreaded tuberculosis, but a small number of patients recovered while in the sanatorium's healthy atmosphere.

Katherine did everything she could to make her visits interesting. She didn't dare kiss Julius because she might contract the disease. She pushed him a short distance in his rolling chair, telling him about activity at the sawmill and about a couple of the woods hicks he considered friends. She made sure he was comfortable and smoothed his bedclothes, always carefully washing her hands before leaving. Her visit had to be short because her father brought her and took her home, attempting to get back to Helen before dark.

In her last visits, Julius was a mere skeleton. Despite his weakness, he still was able to hold a cloth over his mouth when he coughed. He still was able to whisper, "I love you." Finally he stopped coughing. He stopped opening his eyes and responding to her. She was glad when her dad signaled that it was time to leave.

Julius died almost three years after they married, and Katherine failed to return to the happy young woman she had been when she became his wife. She married much later than most young women because mountain girls married as young as fourteen or fifteen. She had been the old age of nineteen and worried that she would become an old maid. Julius came into her life to make her laugh, and he made her totally happy until his illness consumed them both.

As a widow, she had nothing in common with Helen's youth and resisted all their activities. She stayed alone, reading and sewing, until her parents decided she should move to Atlanta. They arranged to rent a room from Mrs. Eloise Martin, the elderly daughter of a Confederate soldier and an active member of United Daughters of the Confederacy. Katherine and her parents were well acquainted with the UDC because it supported Rabun Gap School, which Katherine had attended.

CHAPTER 3

UMBRELLA

The shopper came out of the little stall and handed Katherine all four dresses. "I'm not taking these," she said.

"Do you like them? Is there any way we can alter them for you?" Katherine said. She was using the word *alter* as if it had always been part of her vocabulary.

"No," the shopper said.

"You know you can make monthly payments on anything you buy here at Rich's." The founder of Rich's believed that each person was inherently honest, and it was a rare shopper who had enough money to pay the total cost of a purchase. Shoppers at Rich's deeply appreciated the ability to buy items by making monthly partial payments. Financial loans from banks had to be repaid in full, not in partial payments.

"I know. Maybe I'll be back later."

After the shopper resisted her efforts to complete the sale, Katherine took the dresses back to the display racks. Looking through all the dresses, she found one she wanted, but it cost too much even though it would be divided into monthly payments.

When her time for lunch arrived, she left the women's wear department and went to the store's basement, which was known for bargains. She always brought lunch to work with her—a biscuit, a piece of chicken, or a piece of fruit—and ate in the dressing room. She never purchased food at the little eatery in the basement and never went upstairs to eat at the store's Magnolia Room, with its snow-white linen tablecloths and exquisite lunch menu.

She couldn't buy lunch when she wanted to put her money into her personal appearance. This time she spent four dollars on a two-piece, navy-blue crepe dress in the popular long-waist style. She was pleased because a similar dress upstairs was almost eight dollars.

Each day passed quickly as Katherine learned that city life was different from mountain life. She made mental notes daily to share her experiences with her mother. She was hurrying to work on another rainy day when a heavy wind caused her to seek shelter in the lobby of a high-class hotel. The wind had blown rain through the door and onto the hotel's marble floor. A man was holding the door open for her as she ran onto the wet surface. Her feet didn't get traction; she slid, lost her balance, and landed prostrate underneath a large, exquisitely carved, wooden table.

The man at the door immediately jumped to help her. After she crawled out, she took his hand and pulled herself upright. Her dress was wet on one side, her umbrella was crushed, and her handbag was dripping. She was too embarrassed to notice the pain in her bruised knee and hip.

"Are you hurt?" he said.

"No, and I must get to work," she said.

"You don't have an umbrella now, and it's still pouring rain."

"I'll go into the ladies' room here and dry off. Maybe the rain will stop."

In the restroom, an attendant offered her a small towel, and she stepped into a stall for privacy. Her soft muslin slip with its delicately embroidered bodice was as wet as her silk-and-cotton crepe dress. She dried both garments on the inside and outside. She was able to remove enough water to stop them from clinging to her body. She thoroughly wiped her embossed leather handbag and took out a nickel to give to the attendant before going back to the lobby where the man was waiting.

"I have an umbrella for you," he said. "You can return it to me later."

Katherine didn't like taking his umbrella but felt she had no choice. "Where do I return it?"

"Just leave it at the desk here for C. S. Callahan," he said. "Can you tell me your name?"

"I'm Katherine Sheldon," she said before taking the umbrella. C. S. Callahan looked like a businessman, and Katherine wondered where he might work.

He held the door open once again, and she walked stiffly onto the sidewalk. Throughout the morning, Katherine felt that shoppers immediately saw her damp clothes and knew about her clumsiness, but she was completely dry that afternoon. The rain had completely stopped when she walked to the streetcar, stopping at the hotel to leave the umbrella for C. S. Callahan. The hotel clerk thanked her and asked no questions. Katherine didn't know that Callahan would become a major figure in her life.

At Mrs. Martin's small four-room house, she changed quickly into a blue cotton dress. Supper was served exactly at seven o'clock each evening, and Mrs. Martin handed her a letter from her mother before exclaiming about her good luck earlier in the afternoon.

"A farm wagon came down the street this morning, and I was able to get green beans, okra, fresh corn, and a cantaloupe," Mrs. Martin said as Katherine sat down. Arthritis caused Mrs. Martin to stop tending her small garden, but she still grew tomatoes and cucumbers. Katherine passed her plate to be filled with the vegetables and a piece of corn bread.

She was glad Mrs. Martin served water to drink instead of the strange sweet iced tea they served in Rich's Magnolia Room. She had purchased a glass of the tea after hearing the other clerks talk about it, but she didn't like it at all. It was too sweet and looked like a watery mixture of the Black Draught medicine her mother had once given her.

"Fresh vegetables weren't my only good luck today. I enjoyed the meeting of our women's group." Mrs. Martin was talking about the United Daughters of the Confederacy. The group had organized in southern states more than thirty years earlier to decorate Confederate graves, perpetuating "the memory of Confederate heroes and the glorious cause for which they fought."

The Atlanta group donated money to Rabun Gap School to help mountain children, and Katherine had loved the school. Now the Atlanta group was accepting obligations that came with voting rights for women. They were casually discussing candidates for public office.

Mrs. Martin was widowed early in life by her much older husband, who was a veteran of the Mexican-American War, and she had no children. She worked in the Southern Railway office and never remarried. On retirement, she received a monthly check from the railway company as well as a small monthly check from her husband's military service.

In addition to her small home, she owned a green 1928 Ford Model A roadster, with yellow wire wheels. She was very proud of her automobile, and her steady income and previous years as an executive secretary left her rather outspoken, not afraid to state her opinion.

Katherine tried to show interest in Mrs. Martin's words, especially when she said that the City of Atlanta was not able to pay its teachers, and Rich's Department Store was cashing their worthless checks without requiring them to spend money at Rich's.

Money wasn't circulating at all in most of Georgia, and banks were failing. But some Atlantans, including Katherine and Mrs. Martin, weren't feeling this severe drawback of the Great Depression.

"We're joining Atlanta businessmen next week to talk about the candidates, and I want you to go with me as my guest," Mrs. Martin said.

After learning the exact date and time, Katherine told her she could meet her at the gathering. She would not be working late hours that Saturday and could get there as the meeting began. Her presence would please Mrs. Martin, and Katherine's parents would be pleased when they learned about it.

Mrs. Martin then asked her to join her on Sunday afternoon to visit her old sick friend, Mary Annie Jackson, and her family. Katherine quickly agreed to go.

After supper, dishes were washed, the radio was turned on, and Mrs. Martin settled down beside it to listen to the new and popular Jack Benny program. Katherine liked to listen to any program simply to hear the pronunciation of words. All her life, she had listened to her mother stress proper speaking style, and she was constantly aware of her own articulation.

She didn't listen this time, but went to her tiny room to read her mother's letter.

Dear Katherine,

> Your old room is occupied again by Angel, Hank, and Hank Jr. We invited them to join us because Hank no longer has a job. He was in the last group to lose work with the sawmill.
> He's trying to find work in Cleveland, but no luck yet. He has made it known that he will do any kind of hard labor, but nothing is available. He got a short job placing a Coca-Cola advertising picture on a large billboard in Cleveland. He had to stand on a platform and use a big brush to push huge pieces of the picture over the structure. He had to make sure each piece exactly matched the other piece, and I think he enjoyed the feeling of being creative. I wish he could get such a job, but, of course, billboards are rare.
> Angel is a good mother, and John and Joe enjoy looking after Hank Jr. now and then. Maybe he'll play with them when he's old enough to walk, but there's such a difference in their ages.
> All Fannie Mae's boys have left and gone up north. I know they had to do that to find some kind of job, but Fannie Mae and Stretch miss them so much. I wish she had at least one daughter.

Please write to me as often as you can and tell me what you are doing. We also hope you are making new friends.

With love,
Mom and Daddy

Katherine's father had persuaded her mother to accept Hank after Angel secretly married him. Katherine's parents considered Angel Rigsby a sister of Katherine. Katherine could barely remember the time when she wasn't with them.

Hank was eight years older than Angel, and Katherine understood her mother's first opposition to him. She had her own bad memories of Hank when she was a second grader and he was a fifth grader at their school.

She told Angel how young Hank took her in bushes behind the school, pulled down her drawers, and held her as he kissed her body, but Angel did not lose her fascination with Hank. He had grown up in Detroit and was totally different from the other young men in Helen.

Her mother said in her previous letter that the sawmill equipment was being shipped to Mexico. There was no hope of someone operating it again.

The huge mill was the reason the little town of Helen existed. Slow production and short working hours caused many of the families to leave. Now the mill was gone. What was going to happen to the few families who were still there? What would become of the town?

CHAPTER 4

HER EYES

Sunday afternoon came quickly, and Katherine was in for a surprise.

Mrs. Martin carried a fresh cake, and Katherine carried one of her own handmade dresses. She had no closet in her little room, and her store-bought dresses were beginning to fill the room's wall space.

Mrs. Martin knew Mrs. Jackson had a daughter the same size as Katherine, so Katherine hoped the daughter would like the dress.

Mary Annie Jackson lived a few miles away, and the muddy dirt roads caused slow travel, but Mrs. Martin was unfazed. They passed rows of small houses with black people on the front porches, and Mrs. Martin parked in front of the Jackson house. Old tin cans of all sizes containing potted plants and flowers completely lined the outer edge of the porch. Two figures, Mary Annie's husband, Will, and his neighbor, were sitting in two old straight-back chairs.

Will left the porch and took the cake as Mrs. Martin got out of her car. A large dog came around the house to greet them, and Mrs. Martin offered it a piece of corn bread from her basket.

After the initial greeting inside the house, Mary Annie called to her daughter, "Dinah Sue, please come here."

A tall, young black woman with skin much lighter than her mom's entered the room. "I want you to meet my new friend from the mountains. This is Katherine Sheldon," said Mary Annie.

Katherine looked at Dinah Sue just as Dinah Sue looked at her, and Katherine looked away quickly. She was afraid to look back, afraid her eyes would betray her.

Dinah Sue began talking, but Katherine still couldn't look. Finally she looked back into the beautiful bright blue eyes of the caramel-colored face.

Dinah Sue was asking her about her job at Rich's, and Katherine quickly explained her work.

"I'm engaged to a man who is graduating next spring from Morehouse College. I'm graduating too, from Spelman College, and we're going to New York City. I hope I can get a job there like you have," Dinah Sue said. Katherine was pleased that the young woman and her fiancé would graduate from Atlanta's universities established for black students. Other colleges and universities did not allow black students.

"I hope you can too, if that's what you want," Katherine said. The young woman would stand out in any place, and maybe New Yorkers would accept her.

Katherine had not recalled the color of the dress she brought and was surprised to see that it was exactly the color of Dinah Sue's eyes. When she offered it, Dinah Sue squealed with delight. "I'll use this as my going-away dress," she said.

When the visit concluded, and Katherine was back in the car with Mrs. Martin, she said, "I wonder how the Jackson family is able to live so well. I guess Mr. Jackson makes a good salary."

"Oh, Mary Annie worked for a wonderful white family. When she became unable to work, they continued to pay her. She still gets a salary although she's bedridden. Will is a porter on the railroad, and he does well."

"I wish all black women could get that kind of job. I was surprised to see Dinah Sue's blue eyes. Did Will ever speak about that to you?"

"Yes, people never forget Dinah Sue, and some of Will's best friends are afraid of her."

"What did Will say about her eyes?"

"He was as surprised as anyone when they became blue. She was only two days old when they got her, so her eyes didn't have their permanent color."

"She's adopted?"

"Yes, Will and his wife adopted two children. I'm sure you know that white men regularly call on young colored women."

Katherine shook her head negatively, and Mrs. Martin went on. "A white man stops his car in front of a colored woman's house and toots the horn. She walks out and joins him for a couple of hours, a night, or a few days. The woman is usually paid well. Colored people have started referring to white people now as "honkies." It's because the white man honks his horn for pleasure with a colored woman."

Katherine didn't know what to say. She didn't know that Georgia law forbade marriage of a white and black couple. Georgia didn't go as far as neighboring Florida, which stated that any white and black couple who spent the night in the same room would go to prison for twelve months or be fined $500.

"They had a handsome colored son much older than Dinah Sue, but he was stabbed to death about ten years ago. They know who stabbed him, and they know nothing will be done about it. The police never investigate the murder of a colored person."

CHAPTER 5

STOP AT BOB'S

The meeting of the UDC came quickly, and Katherine was surprised that it was held at Atlanta's Municipal Auditorium, the largest gathering place available.

After work, Katherine put on her hat and gloves and walked to the auditorium where she easily found Mrs. Martin, who was standing just inside the entryway. Immediately she began introducing Katherine to other members of the UDC. She liked to explain her friends' membership credentials, saying, "This is Mrs. Doyle, whose father died at Chickamauga; Mrs. Cunningham, whose uncle survived prison in Fort Delaware; and Miss Coopwood, whose much older brother fought in the Battle of Sharpsburg."

The large auditorium was filled with businessmen, and Mrs. Martin and her UDC friends appeared to be the only females. Katherine saw no other female her age and was still meeting Mrs. Martin's friends when a man on the stage used the microphone to call the meeting to order and introduce the Atlanta mayor.

The mayor said they would hear from candidates seeking the position of Georgia governor, as well as Franklin Delano Roosevelt, governor of New York, who had been named the presidential nominee for the Democratic Party. Roosevelt was there in person. He was appearing in every state possible to prove that he was strong and energetic although his body had been damaged by polio.

Katherine and the UDC members sat in a group at the back of the auditorium, and Katherine found it hard to concentrate on the speakers. Ten men, including Eugene Talmadge, were running for governor and seeking the support of the Democratic Party. Six of the gubernatorial candidates spoke, but Talmadge wasn't there. A Talmadge supporter went to the mike, said a few words, and then sang, "Got a Eugene dog, got a Eugene cat. I'm a Talmadge man from my shoes to my hat. Farmer in the cornfield hollering 'Whoa, gee, haw. Can't put no thirty-dollar tag on my three-dollar car.'"

Mrs. Martin whispered to her that Talmadge promised to reduce the cost of car tags to three dollars. "He also said he was going to appear only in counties where the streetcars don't run," she said. In other words, he would campaign only in farm counties.

Despite attempts to be interested in the remarks, Katherine was beginning to feel drowsy. She watched Roosevelt limp to the microphone on crutches, but she couldn't stay alert as he talked about a "new deal." He talked about the Depression and his voice grew louder as he said, "The country needs and, unless I mistake its temper, the country demands bold, persistent experimentation. It is common sense to take a method and try it. If it fails, admit it frankly and try another. But above all, try something."

After a round of loud applause and cheers, he left the auditorium. Katherine was thinking about the words "Above all, try something," when another man walked onto the stage and said he could answer questions concerning Franklin Roosevelt. She didn't look toward him until he said his name was Chris Callahan. He was the man who had helped her at the hotel and loaned her an umbrella.

She was quite surprised that he was from New York. Although she had lived an isolated life in the mountains, she knew that New Yorkers and all Yankees laughed and poked fun at Georgians. Young men in Helen who joined the army told her how people in New York laughed at them, teased them about their language, and said they lived on fatback and sorghum syrup, and never wore shoes.

The Civil War had ended almost seventy years earlier, but the North and the South still were passionately at odds. The North was enjoying a new sophistication where colored people could get somewhat better jobs, and Yankee journalists considered the South an intellectual and cultural wasteland. Radio programs and movies made Georgia and the entire South the butt of all jokes. The constant ridicule made the South rebellious and withdrawn as much as before the Civil War.

Katherine didn't know if she should speak to Mr. Callahan but decided she must make sure his umbrella had been returned to him. A group gathered around him when the meeting concluded, and she slowly made her way to him.

She was wearing her beige wedge heels, and he still was almost two inches taller. The heat of the crowd caused him to remove his slate-colored suit jacket, and his shoulders remained broad under a white short-sleeved shirt. His black hair, parted on the left side, was smoothed back from a tan forehead. His long tie was red, white, and blue.

"You were kind to lend me your umbrella last week. I left it at the hotel, and I hope it was returned to you."

"Oh, hello, Katherine Sheldon. Please tell me where you work."

He remembered her name. Why did he want to know her place of employment? Did he not get his umbrella? After a pause, she answered, "I work at Rich's. Thank you for lending me your umbrella."

Another man pushed his way into a conversation with Callahan, and Katherine turned away. She didn't have time to ask him again about his umbrella and hurried to join Mrs. Martin as it was almost midnight. Together they caught the last streetcar home.

The following week was routine, except that Elliot Jones, supervisor of the women's wear department, resigned. He wasn't replaced, and the three clerks worked diligently to keep everything in order.

On Friday evening, Katherine stepped from Rich's onto the sidewalk and was immediately stopped by a young man. She was surprised to see that it was Chris Callahan. "May I buy you a Coca-Cola?" he said.

"Thank you, but I must get home." She would barely make the seven o'clock supper.

"I'll take you home, and it won't take long to drink a Coke."

Katherine was afraid, but she didn't know what she feared. Callahan didn't look dangerous, but she felt vulnerable where males were concerned. Her future success must never again depend on a man. It wouldn't take long to join him for a soda, but she couldn't respond and only looked at him silently.

He took her arm and guided her a few steps to a car. He opened the door and seated her in the front.

"What kind of car is this?" Katherine's mind was working again, and she knew her father would ask her later.

"A Dodge Tourer," he said. "It's four years old but in good shape, and it will haul six people in comfort. It's what I needed. Where do you want to stop for a soda?"

"We can stop at Bob's. It's close to my room."

Bob's was a soda fountain in the corner of a general store near Mrs. Martin's house. Callahan pulled into the nearest parking place, and they went into the building to find a table. A man came to them after they were seated, and Callahan ordered a Coke while Katherine ordered a NuGrape.

"I've never tried a NuGrape. How is it?" Callahan said, looking at her glass of purple liquid.

"It's carbonated, but really smooth and has a grape juice flavor." Words from a NuGrape radio advertisement suddenly popped into her mind, and she said, smiling, "The flavor dances around on my taste buds."

Callahan responded with an engaging chuckle that soothed Katherine's nerves as she noticed the twinkle in his brown eyes.

"I have to get to my room because supper is served at seven o'clock," she said.

"I hope you can help me learn more about the people of Atlanta because I'm working in Georgia during Roosevelt's campaign," Callahan said.

"I'm sorry, but I don't know the people in Atlanta. I'm new here, and I really can't help you."

"Where are you from?" he said, sipping his Coke.

Katherine told him that she was from the small town of Helen north of Atlanta, but with the sawmill now gone, she had no idea what was going to happen to the town.

"Helen and the mountain towns are important to the Roosevelt campaign. I see that you aren't wearing a wedding ring, and I hope you'll tell me about your life and what brought you to Atlanta."

"My husband died, and my parents wanted me to live in Atlanta so I could learn to live without him. I'm enjoying my work at Rich's, but I look forward to going back home."

"I'll have to deliver you to your supper, but please tell me when I can see you again. Do you have plans for Sunday?" Callahan said as he placed her in the front seat of his car again.

"I go to church Sunday morning and evening."

"May I pick you up Sunday afternoon for a short drive? We can explore Atlanta together, and it will help me to have someone with me."

Katherine was silent again, hesitating to say yes.

"I'll pick you up about two o'clock. We'll visit casual spots, and you don't have to wear anything special."

Katherine pointed out Mrs. Martin's house. He stopped, hurried around to open the car door for her, walked her to the house, and again opened the door for her.

"I'll see you Sunday," he said, and she only lifted her hand in farewell without answering.

At the supper table, Mrs. Martin became excited when she told her about one of Roosevelt's campaign staffers bringing her home.

"Roosevelt may be the governor of New York, but he spends a lot of time in Georgia at Warm Springs, and his wife's paternal grandmother was Mittie Roosevelt, who lived in Roswell. The Democratic Party adopted his New Deal ideas at the same time they named him the nominee. Franklin Delano Roosevelt will be the best president Georgia could have," Mrs. Martin said.

CHAPTER 6

CYCLORAMA

On Sunday, Katherine dressed for church, intending to wear the same clothes if Callahan came to pick her up. She put on a simple, handmade cotton blouse with a gray cotton pleated skirt. Her close-fitting velveteen hat, made by her mother, was decorated with a silk grosgrain ribbon and small bird feathers.

He appeared as promised, said hello to Mrs. Martin, and escorted Katherine to his car.

Callahan said he hoped she wanted to visit the Cyclorama. "I am fascinated by the War between the States. Some of the stories are exciting, and some are very sad," he said. "My ancestors came over from Ireland, and they had enough wars there. They didn't want to get involved again."

The Cyclorama had been created almost sixty years earlier and was placed in a new building after Georgia and Atlanta began believing in the South's "Lost Cause," promoted by the United Daughters of the Confederacy.

Katherine had heard talk about the Cyclorama so she wanted to see it too. Callahan passed a portion of Grant Park Zoo and found a parking place nearby.

Once inside, he bought their tickets and were told they would have to wait about an hour before the next volunteer guide was available. They began touring the Civil War museum and went downstairs to see the locomotive called "Texas."

Katherine wasn't sure Callahan knew the details about Confederate Civil War history. "Do you know about the train race?" she said. He didn't.

"The Union Army commandeered a locomotive called 'The General' with plans to take it from here to Chattanooga and tear up the railroad tracks all the way. Confederate soldiers chased them on foot and later chased them in this locomotive, 'The Texas.' They finally captured them. I saw it all in a movie called *The General*."

"I wish I'd seen the movie," he said.

After looking at war uniforms, weapons, and historical papers, they walked into a large circular stage that was completely surrounded by a huge oil painting on canvas. Their guide announced that if the painting were placed on a flat surface, it would be 42 feet high and 358 feet long, "the world's largest oil painting."

It was created with input from Union and Confederate soldiers as well as a man who followed Gen. William Sherman, who ordered the burning of Atlanta. It depicted a site east of the city at the Georgia Railroad and inside Union lines.

The artwork was superb, and a three-dimensional matching scene, a diorama, tilted into the bottom of the painting. Actual red dirt that matched the painting was filled with artificial shrubs and 128 plaster figures of soldiers. The tour guide said the size of the human figures varied from twenty inches to fifty inches tall to fit in perspective with the scale of the painting. Some of the figures held guns in a fighting position, and others represented dead or wounded soldiers. Some figures were in blue uniforms, and some were in gray uniforms. The diorama flowed into the painting with no visible connection. It portrayed the battle of Atlanta on July 22, 1864.

It was bleak and sad. Katherine liked Atlanta's current tall buildings and bustling lifestyle. The Cyclorama represented months of creative artwork by a large number of people. But the scenes and images depicted a history of mankind that was disturbing.

She knew war was necessary sometimes to prevent one group of people from doing great harm to another group. But today she didn't want to believe Atlanta ever looked like the scenes around her. She liked a comment made decades earlier by Varina Howell Davis, wife of Jefferson Davis, president of the Confederacy. She said if women had had the right to vote, maybe the Civil War wouldn't have taken place.

As they walked out, Callahan asked Katherine if she lost an ancestor in the war. "No. I went to a boarding school where we constantly had arguments about the Civil War. One student argued that her family never owned slaves, but her great-grandfather and four of his sons died fighting in the Confederacy. They were trying to protect their home from the Yankees. We knew slavery was the reason for the war, and we argued about whether our nation's Constitution approved slavery. I think it wasn't approval because it counted slaves as three-fifths of a person, not three-fifths of a property."

Callahan said, "My ancestors fought in wars in Ireland, and please don't think I'm a coward, but I don't understand war. You know how we are shocked today at the idea of cannibalism. Well, I think people in the distant future will be shocked by war."

"You talk like my dad," Katherine said.

They were thinking of a war acted out with men using guns to shoot at each other. They didn't want to recall the recent news that had excited some people, stories about airplanes with machine guns. They had not yet experienced the horror that started before World War II, the massacre of thousands of innocent Jewish men, women, and children. The Japanese airplanes hadn't yet bombed Pearl Harbor, and the atomic bomb had not yet been created.

Callahan wanted to change the subject. "Atlanta was burned because it was a vital distribution hub for ammunition during the Civil War." He smiled. "Today, Atlanta's a vital distribution hub for Coca-Cola." They both chuckled.

Leaving the building, he asked Katherine if she could go to the zoo. It didn't take long to see the small collection of animals donated by different citizens, and they looked longer at the monkeys, which were picking fleas from each other or picking food from a few bananas that had been thrown into their cage.

"I've told you I don't like war, and I don't like to see animals kept in cages," Callahan said as they got in his car. "Some people would say I'm not being a man, but I read that President Abraham Lincoln felt the same way."

"There once was a black bear kept in a small building on a farm near Helen. The building was so small the bear could barely turn around. It's always made me sad to think about it," said Katherine.

"Tell me more about Helen. It's a sawmill town, but that's all I know."

"It was a wonderful place to grow up. It makes me sad that it will someday be gone. My mother worked at a restaurant in the Mountain Ranch Hotel, and I worked there too. A lot of people visited there from Atlanta and other distant places. The hotel once had four hundred people staying there at the same time. Some of them had to sleep on the porches."

"What's it like now?"

"The hotel is still busy, but many people are gone, and the trees are gone too. My dad says we should keep our faith and adjust to change, so I'm trying to adjust."

"What kind of work does your dad do?"

"He's the preacher at a Helen church, and it's time for me to get home and get ready to go to my church here."

"I'll get you home, but when can I see you again?"

Callahan already was approaching Mrs. Martin's house. He soon opened her car door, helped her out, and escorted her to the door. He said, "I'll be waiting for you one day when you leave work."

Katherine thanked him again before entering the house. She hoped she would see him again soon because his comments made her think and use her head. Suddenly she knew she wanted her life to count for something. *My life must have a purpose. I must give something back for the space I'm occupying here on this earth.*

Mrs. Martin expressed pleasure once again that she had spent time with someone who was working for Roosevelt. Katherine didn't tell her that Chris Callahan had not once said anything about the presidential candidate.

CHAPTER 7

NO ONE TO MOURN

On Monday evening, Katherine was pleased to get another letter from her mother. She finished supper with Mrs. Martin and helped clear the supper dishes before going to her room to read it.

Dearest Daughter,

Your father insisted on taking me to see our old homeplace. I knew the road wasn't good, but truly I was afraid to go and felt guilty because I had been away so long. After all, it's been twenty years. But we finally went, and I felt so lost. We drove through stumpland all the way to our old home, and I looked forward to arriving in Spring Cove on Tray Mountain where my parents always celebrated the mountains' natural beauty. But the trees are gone there too. We didn't see a single wild animal on the entire trip, not even a bird. My childhood is gone. All the precious reminders of my parents are gone. Everything disappeared, and no one was there to mourn the departure.

The old log cabin my daddy built is there, but the door was standing open. Someone evidently lived there sometime during our absence, and everything was torn and dirty. Under the settee cushions, I found an old piece of paper with the words "Jim loves Ellie." This tells me that the two men who killed both Angel's daddy and Cousin Melvin lived in our cabin. They were hung for the murder of Angel's daddy, and poor Ellie is gone now too, without ever finding the happiness she was seeking. There's no point in worrying about them now.

I didn't want to stay because there was no shade, only sadness. I left there long ago thinking I would return in three years. I thought constantly of returning until I became responsible for our house in Helen. At first, I only wanted to keep our Helen house perfect for when Dorothy returned. Then I thought constantly of making the house a home. I completely abandoned the dear old homeplace and forgot that I was responsible for it.

Since we visited, your dad learned that the lumber company placed notes on the cabin's door several times but never learned who was responsible for the place. The company learned that taxes were owed, paid them, became the owner, and cut all the trees.

When you and I were there, life was good. The trees were a major part of our existence. They gave us the seasons. Their blooms and varied shades of green gave us spring. They gave us shade in the summer. They colored their leaves red and yellow to give us autumn. They even helped us in winter by dropping their leaves to let the warming sun shine through. The trees owned the mountains, and now the mountains are abandoned.

When we lived there, we celebrated the beauty of the mountains that God created for us. Now there is no beauty to celebrate.

I've used this letter to you to moan about my sadness. Before I began writing, I felt as if the goodness of our mountains and my childhood had been sucked from my heart. But the wonderful memories are still there. You have been a bright spot in my life since the minute you were born. Now writing to you has helped me. I'll write a happier letter next time.

I hope you have made new friends. Please write soon and tell me about your life.

With love,
Mom

The letter made Katherine sad and gave her another deep wish. She wanted to restore the majesty of her mother's old homeplace, but there was no way.

Maybe she could find a forest somewhere else and build a cabin there. But although she had a job and a salary, a widowed woman couldn't buy land, and she didn't have the strength to build a cabin herself. A single woman was almost helpless in making major changes, but at least she could vote as soon as she registered.

CHAPTER 8

MOUNTAINS' TREES

The Ku Klux Klan, the secret organization promoting white supremacy, was a big part of conversations during the next week at work.

Slavery still was a dark shadow over Georgia and all southern states. Progressive newspaper editors talked of a New South, but much of Georgia feared change and wanted to keep the Old South.

Laws prohibited any kind of integration between blacks and whites and were referred to as Jim Crow laws. The name came from a popular song-and-dance caricature by a white man in black face called "Jump Jim Crow." The laws maintained white supremacy.

Black Georgians couldn't get jobs, couldn't vote, and absolutely could not mix with white people except to do chores for paltry pay. The laws controlled every aspect of life for blacks and whites.

The Ku Klux Klan had lost membership in the last years and was trying to rebuild. A march was expected to take place on Peachtree Street on Saturday. The secret organization had made national news ten years earlier when it fired a sculptor who was supposed to commemorate the KKK and the South's "Lost Cause" on the side of a gigantic hunk of granite called Stone Mountain. Now the carving depicted only the head of Lee, and no one seemed to know any person who was a KKK member.

Katherine's information about the Klan was only what she heard in casual conversations. She knew of no statement from an official source. She knew the organization used intimidation and violence to promote white supremacy. It used Bible scripture and claimed it was following God's wishes. Katherine knew it had been active during the Reconstruction years after the Civil War.

She also knew what her father had said about the Klan: "It claims to promote the traditional American family, but it actually promotes hate. It says that only white American Protestant men are worthy. Its members sometimes do horrible things to an individual they don't agree with. They do most of their work during night hours, and some KKK members should be sent to prison."

Now the Klan was expected to march, and no one knew how big the march was going to be. Katherine didn't plan to see the event because she would be working.

On Saturday morning, one of the early shoppers talked about seeing a group of figures in white sheets and cone hats gathering near the new Fox Theater, which was more than a mile north of Rich's. It was almost noon before a customer said the march was slowly trickling toward Rich's on the sidewalk. Not enough costumed KKK members had shown up to close the street.

All three women's wear clerks were consumed with curiosity. "We need to see what the fuss is about," said Roseanne, the oldest clerk. Customers had stopped coming in the store, and the clerks agreed to go one by one and look for a minute. They had to go downstairs to the Peachtree Street door, which took another couple of minutes.

Katherine was the last one to go, and she stepped outside the front door just as three sheeted stragglers walked by carrying a Confederate flag. A conical head turned toward her and a man's voice said, "Our way is the Christian way, the law-and-order way, the way of love for family and nation." Suddenly the voice added, "Get back to work."

Katherine stepped back inside and hurried to her workstation. She'd heard the man's voice before but couldn't place it. She had to think about his words. *If they are Christians, why are they keeping their membership a secret? Christians are supposed to love all mankind.*

Hanging dresses, cleaning and arranging displays kept her busy throughout the afternoon, as customers were few. Sunday passed quickly, and on Monday, work activity returned to normal. As Katherine left work, Chris Callahan once again approached her.

"I was too busy to come by last week, but I hope you can join me again for a quick soda," he said. He had a big smile and obviously was expecting her to say yes. She nodded her head, not able to say no.

He guided her to his car and once again they traveled toward Bob's. In the car, she said, "I've told you about my life and growing up in Helen. Please tell me about your life."

"Oh, I grew up in a very quiet Georgia town called Chipley."

"I thought you were from New York."

"No, I've never even visited New York. I'm active in the University of Georgia alumni association, and Governor Roosevelt asked me to help him with his campaign for president. I met him when he was at Warm Springs."

Katherine would learn that Chipley was in west central Georgia on the northern edge of Harris County where it joins Meriwether County. Decades later, after a rich family built the beautiful Callaway Gardens at Chipley, its name would be changed to Pine Mountain. Warm Springs was only about ten miles away.

"I'm surprised. I'm glad to know you're from Georgia, but I don't know anything about political campaigns. I've never even voted."

As they were sipping a Coke and a NuGrape, he said, "I have some information about Helen and trees in the Georgia mountains. Governor Roosevelt wants to hire people to plant trees if he's elected."

"He'll have to plant millions of trees if he wants to replace the trees in our mountains," Katherine said with a touch of sarcasm.

"I found information about Georgia trees in the *Atlanta Constitution*. I copied it so I could ask you if it was correct before I send it to headquarters." Callahan handed her a sheet of paper, and its ink odor reminded her of the mimeograph machine at Rabun Gap School.

Katherine glanced at it but couldn't absorb its words. "My mother's last letter is about the trees," she said.

"If the letter is about the trees, please bring it to work with you tomorrow morning. I can have it copied and will give it back to you in the afternoon."

"It's only about her sadness. I don't know if I should share it," Katherine said.

"I promise you that Governor Roosevelt is concerned about the forests being destroyed. The lack of trees is causing a lot of damage. It's too much to explain now. If your mother's letter will help in replacing the trees, she'll be glad."

"Take me to my room, and let me read this," she said, indicating the mimeograph sheet. "Maybe I can bring Mom's letter to you in the morning."

Callahan drove her to Mrs. Martin's in time for her to hurry to the supper table. She hadn't yet read the mimeographed paper that he gave her and told Mrs. Martin about his request to copy her mother's letter. Mrs. Martin read her mom's letter and told her she definitely should take it to Callahan the next morning.

Later in her room, she read the mimeograph sheet given to her by Callahan. It was from an *Atlanta Constitution* article dated more than forty years earlier. Headlined "Away Up in the Northeast," the article's writer said that not much was known about the northeastern part of Georgia, but it would grow when people were able to visit.

> It is the garden spot of Georgia.
>
> This section has a few things of which it can truthfully boast. The first thing I mention is its timber ... You can see scores of yellow poplar in its coves measuring from 20 to 30 feet in circumference ...
>
> They can be seen by the thousands, trees 50 to 60 feet high before a limb is seen. I can point out to you in Union County hundreds of trees of this kind, so many feet in diameter that the huge circular saw on exhibition at the Piedmont fair could not saw without first quartering them. Not the poplar only, but in the same and adjoining coves you will find an abundance

of buckeye, wild cherry, walnut, mulberry, and last, but not least, mahogany—I mean what I say, mahogany.

The mountaineers call the tree "mountain bay," but it's as pure mahogany as ever grew in South America.

Northeast Georgia has been considered poverty-stricken—lands poor and not worth the labor expanded in cultivation. I admit all that is said about her in this respect, but she is fabulously rich in timber and minerals. But our people do not realize it—others do.

The article went on to encourage the newspaper's readers to invest in sawmills or minerals.

Katherine knew that men from the Midwest had built the Helen sawmill. She also knew that Northeast Georgia once had valuable minerals and experienced a gold rush seventy or eighty years before the sawmill was built. Thousands of men came from distant places and joined local men, and the peaceful Cherokee Indians were driven out.

Combined efforts to gain quick wealth sometimes almost destroyed the mountains. Dynamite and hydraulic mining—using high-pressure jets of water to remove the earth—left massive red ditches, and long, deep tunnels were dug, but no one ever got rich.

This mimeograph told her about the trees that were gone. Any person in Helen could tell Chris Callahan about the trees. He didn't need an old newspaper article. She didn't know why her mother's letter would help, but Mrs. Martin insisted that Katherine share it with him.

The next morning, she prepared to take the letter to work with her and found Callahan waiting for her outside Mrs. Martin's house. He immediately asked about the letter, and she handed it to him.

"This newspaper article is accurate, I'm sure," she said. Very little was spoken between them as he drove her to Rich's.

That evening he met her outside Rich's door, handed her the letter, and thanked her. "I'm sending a copy of this on to headquarters," he said.

CHAPTER 9

DARK SIDE

Katharine did not see Callahan again for four weeks and thought he was probably gone from her life. On a cool evening in late September, Elliot Jones, her former boss, met her as she left the store. She couldn't hold back her surprise at seeing him, and he asked her for a date the following Friday evening.

"You have no reason to turn me down now. We don't work together anymore," he said. "I can pick you up here, and we can go see *Dr. Jekyll and Mr. Hyde.*" She had seen previews of the movie and heard so many WSB radio comments about the horror story that she couldn't resist his invitation.

The movie took her breath away more than once. Dr. Jekyll was a handsome man, and the ugly Mr. Hyde was truly a horror. She wondered if all people had a horrible side as Dr. Jekyll said. Then, thinking of her parents, she told herself no.

After the movie, a newsreel showed Babe Ruth shouting fiery words back at Chicago fans before he hit a homer in the World Series between the Chicago Cubs and the New York Yankees. A Mickey Mouse "Silly Symphony" production called "Flowers and Trees" followed. It was the first time Katherine had seen a color cartoon, and it was filled with dancing, singing trees. She left the theater consumed with thoughts about trees, her mother's letter, and the treeless mountains.

NEW BEGINNINGS

As they shared reactions to the movie, Jones drove her to The Varsity on North Avenue, a restaurant near the Georgia Tech campus. Her coworkers had talked about the restaurant and its clever carhops, and she wanted to see and hear them.

A carhop wearing Number 21 jumped on the back bumper of their car as they drove in. "What'll ya have?" he said to them as soon as the car stopped. They ordered two chili dogs with mustard and onions on the side, french fries, and chocolate milk drinks on ice.

The carhop repeated the order, "Two dogs sideways, with strings, and two PCs." All the words easily described the order except "two PCs." Jones said PC stood for pure chocolate, the milk drink served on ice.

Katherine laughed out loud, and Jones told her the language helped them fill the orders quicker. "Should we develop a language of our own for women's dresses?" she asked, still laughing.

He laughed slightly before saying, "It's good to see these bozos working."

"I have a wonderful colored friend back in Helen. She is practically a member of our family," Katherine said, thinking about Fannie Mae.

"Sure. Colored people were members of families back when they were slaves. They had to work then or answer to their owners."

"My friend was never a slave, and she works as hard as my mother."

"Well, she's unusual. White people have to make sure colored people work or they just lay around. I'm working now for a new printing company, and a big black bozo has applied for a job there twice. They won't hire him, but he refuses to get the message. He keeps coming back."

Katherine had not heard words like this before. Fannie Mae and her family were all valued friends of Katherine's mother and father. In fact, Fannie Mae had joined her father's church when it first was organized.

She recalled Fannie Mae's constant worries about her children not having a regular school like the white children. Katherine's family and Fannie Mae's family all knew that putting the colored children with the white children in Helen would cause its own small war.

In Atlanta, she saw two colored women each day going to work as maids in homes of the wealthy. They always sat at the back of the streetcar and evidently worked at different places because one was dressed in a blue uniform and the other in gray. Katharine didn't know that law required them to sit in the back and never sit close to a white person. She also didn't know that the Depression had caused desperate white people to take some of the jobs formerly held by black people.

Katherine also saw colored men and women waiting to enter Rich's to clean after the store closed. These workers wore old clothing that probably came from a missionary center, not shabby, ragged clothing sometimes seen on blacks, but they had jobs. All the colored people she knew were proud of their work.

"All people are equally valuable in God's eyes," she said, repeating words often heard from her father.

"You have to remember that God placed them on a continent far away because they're not like us," Jones said.

As he talked, Katherine suddenly realized who the man was who spoke to her at the KKK march. It was Jones. Now she knew he had sworn a secret oath to promote white supremacy. Before she could think, she said, "Why are you a member of the KKK?"

Her question surprised him. He paused before he answered, his words louder than before. "We are God's chosen people. White people must stay together to protect our families and protect this nation."

Katherine knew the KKK had previously killed colored people and used secretive violence and terror to keep anyone from speaking out against them. She didn't know how to answer him and finally said, "These hot dogs are good, aren't they?"

She and Jones finished their food without another mention of the KKK, and he drove her to her room. After he escorted her to the door, he attempted to kiss her, but she quickly pulled away, thanked him for the evening, and hurried inside. *Elliot Jones confirms Dr. Jekyll's words. He has an ugly side. I hope I never see him again.*

That night she wrote a letter to her parents and included a question asking her daddy what she should do about white people who disliked colored people so much.

CHAPTER 10

THE REGISTRARS

Callahan was at Rich's door again on Monday evening. "I hope you can spend time with me Sunday afternoon. I have a lot I want to tell you. It's important. You can vote for our next president if you go before the voting board this week to register."

Katherine answered quickly, "I can see you about two o'clock like we did before."

That evening she told Mrs. Martin that she wanted to register to vote. "If you're going before the board, I'll go too. I know I should vote," Mrs. Martin said.

They wouldn't be voting in the governor's election because Eugene Talmadge had become the Democratic Party's nominee in the state primary on September 14. No other political party in Georgia had a gubernatorial candidate so he would be the next governor.

They visited the Board of Registrars on Wednesday afternoon. Three men were present who also applied to go before the board, but no other women. The men went through quickly. Katherine and Mrs. Martin were taken at the same time, and a heavily bearded board member asked them, "Do either of you know what you are doing here?"

They each said, "Yes sir."

"Where are your husbands?"

Both Katherine and Mrs. Martin answered, "Deceased."

"I wonder if they like you being here," he said. Then, chuckling, he added, "Just tell me who is running for office."

Mrs. Martin said, "Franklin Delano Roosevelt, governor of New York, is on the Democratic ticket for president with John Nance Garner of Texas as vice president. Herbert Hoover is on the Republican ticket to be reelected president with Charles Curtis of Kansas back again as vice president. Norman Thomas, a native of Ohio, is the Socialist Party nominee again, and William Z. Foster of Massachusetts is on the Communist ticket with James Ford, a colored man, as vice president."

She did not name state candidates because most of them had been elected with Talmadge during the state primary.

"What do you think about a colored man being so presumptuous that he's running for vice president?" the bearded man said, looking at Katherine.

"I don't know anything about this man. I didn't know he was on the ticket until I saw it in the newspaper this week," Katherine said, without directly answering the question.

They asked more questions, and Katherine was relieved that they didn't ask her why she wanted to vote. She didn't dare say she wanted to vote for Roosevelt because he was going to plant trees in the mountains. She didn't know anyone other than herself and her mother who worried about trees. She knew such words would sound foolish to anyone else.

The board member appeared irritated by their presence. He said, "We don't have to ask all our questions." Neither woman knew he was referring to impossible questions used when colored people attempted to register. He seemed to be amused that these two women planned to vote and chuckled again as he gave them a paper to sign, telling them they could vote on Election Day.

That evening Katherine was pleased to have the letter she had been waiting for from her daddy, and it was a long one.

Dear Daughter,

You always ask me good questions. Now you say, "What can I do about white people who don't like colored people and try to block their progress?"

First we must look at all life forms. Different species of all living creatures stick together. Blackbirds stick together. Doves stick together. Indians stick together. Colored people stick together. White people stick together, etc., etc., etc.

White people make the laws and keep colored people out of lawmaking. Many laws prevent colored communities from advancing. Thus, their young people don't have a successful colored person as an outstanding example to follow.

I must say that discrimination has forever been a part of mankind. It was a problem in the time of Jesus. Part of the reason may be because people are afraid. Because we stay with our own kind, we don't get to know people in the other groups.

A general conversation between two strangers today—one white, one colored—almost never happens. Neither introduces himself. Neither says, "How are you today?" or "What about this weather?" They never get to really know one another.

The Bible is clear on what we should do, but as with many issues, the Bible has many words that can be interpreted both ways. Sometimes people pick out a scripture verse that supports what they have already decided. Then they say their decision comes from God.

Luke chapter 10 is very clear about how we should treat people. Here, we find Jesus talking to his disciples. In verse twenty-five, a lawyer asks Jesus,

"What shall I do to inherit eternal life?" Jesus asked him what he thought the law said. The lawyer said the law told him to love the Lord with his whole heart and love his neighbor as himself.

Jesus told him he was right and that was what he should do for eternal life. But the lawyer wasn't satisfied. He said, "But who is my neighbor?"

This is a wonderful question. We think our neighbor lives in the house next door, but that is not what Jesus was saying. He used a parable to explain the definition of neighbor.

He told about a man assaulted by thieves on the road and left for dead. A priest came near and moved to the other side of the road so he wouldn't have to help the injured man. A Levite, who also worked in the tabernacle, came down the road, and he also crossed to the other side. Then a Samaritan, whose people were held in contempt by the Jews, came near, saw the injured man, bandaged his wounds, put him on his beast, took him to an inn, and took care of him. The next day he told the innkeeper that he would pay him to take care of the injured man.

Jesus asked the lawyer which of these three men was a neighbor to the wounded man.

The lawyer answered, "He that showed mercy."

Jesus said, "Go and do likewise."

This scripture tells us we must love all others and show mercy. It's very clear.

Personally objecting to discrimination in today's world may be difficult. If you are confronted by someone saying bad things about another group of people, you can quietly ask why. Listen to them, and ask more questions. Maybe you can make them examine their own prejudice.

Remember that God is love, and always pray that you follow God's will.

I love you,
Dad

PS—I hope you have found a church with a pastor who preaches from the words of Jesus. Pastors must not delve into politics, and nowadays, in the present heated campaign, I wish I could. We must constantly use the scripture as our guide, and all people who want our state to have a high-quality social order—one of justice and compassion—should join a church of Jesus-seekers.

The church you choose should increase your understanding and love of Jesus. The church becomes your second family and can help in times of need. Like our own family, some church members may be flawed. We must always remember that half-breeds, tax collectors, and prostitutes were friends of Jesus.

Katherine read the letter twice. She knew God valued all people equally.

She recognized problems from the KKK, but didn't recognize problems caused by Jim Crow rules because she had never seen blacks living in freedom.

She decided she was not wrong to be concerned about people, such as her former boss and other members of the Klan. She would continue to be friends with black people. She would talk to black people, and she would listen to them. She would always question prejudice. She couldn't do anything else, but she could vote. And she could pray.

The words about church were an irritation. *Haven't I been in church all my life?* She had been attending preaching services with Mrs. Martin but hadn't attended other activities. She had not joined the church and didn't know any of the other members. She knew her dad would say she should become a member of the church and make friends there. *I know Dad's right, but doesn't he know that I'm trying to be successful here in this town, and it takes a lot of effort and concentration?*

She considered his words a few more minutes before deciding, *I know I must show deep gratitude for all my blessings, and if I want to show love for all humans, I guess I should start in the church.*

CHAPTER 11

VOTING DAY

Katherine began to pay attention to every mention of the presidential candidates and was amazed at the bitterness and cattiness. The attitudes were totally new to her sheltered life as the daughter of a small-town church pastor.

She wanted to learn more about Roosevelt, but good information was hard to find. She read newspaper articles and saw signs on the street that said, "If Roosevelt is elected, we will have Sovietism." She assumed this referred to the Soviet Union and communism.

She remembered that in high school she learned communism did away with capitalism, money, and private ownership of property. The words were supposed to frighten, not inform.

Another was a quote from Talmadge, who said, "Roosevelt's 'New Deal' will bring Yankees back to Georgia." She didn't know anything good about Yankees.

Roosevelt promised to end prohibition and bring back alcohol sales, with the sales tax going into federal coffers. The FDR campaign theme song, "Happy Days Are Here Again," was heard everywhere.

And he's going to plant trees, Katherine thought. She felt a little more foolish about her reasoning every day.

The words of President Herbert Hoover, who was running for reelection for the Republican Party, did nothing to encourage her. He said government should not interfere with business and, referring to the Depression, advised that everyone should "weather the storm."

Later, when she saw Callahan on Sunday afternoon, the first thing she said was "I hope you will tell me why you think Roosevelt would be a good president. Surely he will do more than plant trees. I'm registered to vote, and I want to know I've made a wise decision."

Katherine also wanted to encourage others to vote for Roosevelt, but the two women she worked with at Rich's said they didn't intend to register. She knew Mrs. Martin was encouraging her friends in the UDC to vote for Roosevelt.

When they arrived at Grant Park, Callahan escorted her to the nearest picnic table and sat down. "Please don't be bored with what I say because I want our countryside to be healthy again. We have to do it. I want to tell you some of the things that happen when trees are gone," he said.

"Like your mother said in her letter, after the trees are gone, all the animals disappear. Second, the soil on the mountains is no longer held in place by tree roots so it begins to erode and wash away. The erosion destroys the valuable topsoil and ruins the rivers. Third, people must have trees to live, both the living trees and the harvested trees. Harvested trees provide the lumber for building, and living trees provide oxygen for the air we breathe. Roosevelt said trees are the lungs of our earth. Fourth, trees slow floods and storms." Callahan intended to say more, but Katherine surprised him with a question.

"You said Roosevelt would plant trees if he's elected president. How can he possibly replace all the trees in our mountains?" she said.

"He competed against thirteen other candidates for the Democratic nomination back in July, and when he won, he told what he would do. He talked about a million young unemployed men who would fight soil erosion and replenish the earth. He doesn't want to put people on the dole but wants them to have real jobs. They'll do more than plant trees. They'll build roads, dams for flood control, towers to watch for fires, and much more. He wants people to go out and enjoy nature, so they'll build campgrounds. They'll be paid, but they'll have to send most of the money back home to their parents. He says he's restoring both the earth and its people at the same time.

"Georgia's Democratic nominee for governor, Eugene Talmadge, is against Roosevelt's plans because he thinks it will help colored people. Only ten percent of this state's population voted in the primary on September fourteenth, so the majority of our state's citizens didn't vote for Talmadge and don't support him, but he won the state's county unit votes by a landslide," Callahan said.

Georgia's county unit system, which passed in 1917, was designed to keep the rural counties in power. It gave two votes to each of the smallest counties while the three large counties, such as Fulton where Atlanta is located, got only six votes each. The candidate with a plurality of votes in a county got its unit votes. The county unit votes decided the winner.

"What does *wool-hat* mean? I've heard over and over that the wool-hats put Talmadge in office," Katherine said.

"Wool-hats are dirt farmers. It was the farm counties that elected Talmadge. Silk-hats are the townies, people who live and vote in a town or city.

"Talmadge catered to the emotions and fears of the poor, uneducated white voters. Each day his farm workers have gone with him to his house for their midday meal. They give thanks to God and sit around the table eating together in his two-story, twelve-room house. At quitting time, they go to their shacks. Paydays on Talmadge's farm are like other farm paydays. The workers might receive a pittance or be told their pay is withheld to pay a debt to him as the farm owner. These workers don't usually vote, but if they could, they'd probably vote for Talmadge," Callahan said.

Eugene Talmadge didn't promise change. He catered to rural fears while Georgia was suffering the Great Depression, and neither Katherine nor Callahan knew he would go down in history as Georgia's most malicious and bigoted governor.

Katherine didn't see Callahan again before she went to vote for Roosevelt on the second Tuesday in November. She reluctantly paid her one-dollar poll tax and marked her ballot very carefully, expecting someone to oppose her efforts at any minute.

NEW BEGINNINGS

No other woman was present, and she folded the large paper ballot and stuffed it into a box without incident. She didn't have information on any office except the president and vowed she would know more next time.

After the election polls closed, sworn-in ballot counters began work immediately and worked through the night so the final results could be announced late the next day.

Forty million voters across the nation cast ballots that day, and almost thirteen million of the voters were without jobs or any source of income.

Franklin Roosevelt and John Garner won by a landslide, getting almost 92 percent of the votes in Georgia, and Katherine waited with excitement as she wondered what would happen. Other Democratic Party candidates across the nation were swept into both houses of Congress, and the congressional majorities proved vital for Roosevelt's plans.

CHAPTER 12

MR. WOODY

After Roosevelt was declared president, Katherine didn't think about trees being planted in the mountains because she couldn't believe the president's plans could make a difference.

She hardly noticed the Thanksgiving observance because she was concerned about Christmas. She wanted to go home for Christmas, but sales at Rich's increased for the holidays, and the women's wear clerks were asked to cancel all their days off. She decided she would send gifts to each person in her family and make sure they got there before Christmas.

Activities in the store changed so much she didn't have time to feel homesick. Two young women were brought into women's wear to act as live mannequins. One put on a beautiful dress, silk hose, high-heeled shoes, and a soft velour hat. She held matching gloves and stood almost completely still for thirty minutes with only slight shifts in position. Then the other woman replaced her, wearing a different outfit. Each live mannequin had every hair in place and every fingernail painted perfectly.

Now and then, a customer tried to get a model's attention and referred to her as a "dummy." Katherine and the other two clerks always immediately said "live mannequin" to gently correct them.

Customers became more interesting personally as they explained their difficulties in selecting the perfect Christmas presents.

Christmas decorations were everywhere in the stores, and Katherine was enchanted with Rich's window displays. Live mannequins also were in the windows, and some windows featured moving robots, such as the one with Santa putting gifts under the tree. One window was filled with silver bells of all sizes that chimed different Christmas carols.

She bought her mother a pair of silk hose and Angel a velour hat. Her father and two brothers each would get soft, black capeskin gloves. At the last minute, she bought another pair of capeskin gloves for Hank and a chinchilla cloth polo cap for little Hank Jr. with flaps that could be worn over his ears in cold weather.

Rich's provided the small boxes she needed to wrap each gift, and she put them inside a larger box for mailing.

The store was closed on Christmas Day, and Callahan asked to see Katherine after church. He presented her with a navy-blue crepe de chine tie that also could be worn as a scarf. She gave him a necktie with a red and white design on a blue background. She knew he liked to wear red-white- and-blue ties proclaiming his patriotism.

Callahan told her about visiting his parents in Chipley, and she told him how she wished to go home.

"I've got a letter from Mom that you might be interested in, and she said she doesn't mind if I share it. It's about a man in the mountains everyone is talking about." She gave him the letter.

> Dear Katherine,
>
> We have enjoyed your letters about your friends and your work. Needless to say, we are wondering if—and how—Roosevelt is going to do all the things he has promised.
>
> I am hearing all kinds of stories about a man who lives across the mountain, but sometimes he travels near us. I think you will find him interesting, and maybe your friend who helps President Roosevelt will find him interesting.

I'm sure you remember that the US government purchased some of the land here in the mountains a few years ago. They call it the Georgia National Forest, and I wish it truly was a forest. The man I want to tell you about is the guard. He watches for fires, trespassers, and poachers. His name is Arthur Woody, but people call him Kingfish.

Despite the fact that so many animals are gone, the mountains still have poachers now and then. People say that Mr. Woody always catches them. It's usually hunters who don't know what they're doing, and Mr. Woody tricks them with fake bear tracks.

Men around here never mention him without laughing about something clever he has done.

He's restocking our deer population, and that's in no way funny. He used his own money to buy five young female deer to go with three bucks he already purchased. He named his new deer Nimble, Nancy, Bunny Girl, Bessie, and Billie. I made a note about the names when I heard them because I thought they were so sweet. He now has a small herd of deer, and he knows each by name.

He also placed a new kind of fish in the streams. He ordered them from far north states. Some say they're speckled trout, and others say they're brook trout. Some say rainbow trout. Whatever they call them, fishermen get excited if they catch one.

He got a small group of men near his home to help him build what some refer to as a wide path from Suches to Wolfpen Gap. He said the government would give money to improve a road but not to build a road. People say he actually got government money more than once to grade that path and make it into an actual road because he said it needed improvement.

I wanted you to know all this before telling you that I met him the other day, and Kingfish is a good nickname. He stopped by the store, and when I heard he was there, I went over. He's a big man, and he doesn't wear shoes. At least he was barefoot when I saw him, and it was a cold day. He didn't wear a uniform from the Forest Service, and I've heard that he refused it. Suspenders held up his pants, and his jacket and shirt were open.

He smiles and laughs a lot, and he said President Roosevelt is going to restore our forest. Hearing him say it made me really believe it. After being there and hearing him, I understand why everyone likes him. He has what is called charisma. I call it charm or a magnetic personality.

I shouldn't say this, but I'm going to. I'm delighted that Mr. Woody, a Georgia mountain man, outfoxes people in the federal government. At least they say he has, and I believe it. Federal government bureaus are filled with Yankees, and you know what awful things they say about Georgians and mountaineers. They don't think we have brains, but our own Kingfish outwitted them.

I hope you like your Christmas present. That's the first time I've tried to make a picture quilt. When you use it, just say, "I'm going to the mountains."

Love, Mom

PS—Your dad agrees with me about Arthur Woody. He says he hopes Mr. Woody can come and speak to our church congregation.

After reading the letter, Callahan said, "This man sounds like someone I want to know. I'll make a copy of this letter and send it to headquarters. Tell me about your picture quilt."

"I haven't got it. I don't know what happened. I'm still hoping it will show up."

CHAPTER 13

PICTURE QUILT

One week after New Year's Day, Katherine found a man waiting for her at Mrs. Martin's house. It was Earnest Hill, a deacon in her father's church.

He began apologizing as she approached. "I'm sorry I didn't get to you sooner. I have let your parents down. Here's your Christmas present." He handed her a large box.

Before Katherine could answer, Mrs. Martin said, "I've told Mr. Hill he can spend the night here before he starts back to the mountains. I have supper ready, so let's eat."

"May I first open this gift?" Katherine said, trying to open the box. Hill handed her his opened pocketknife, and she cut the small cords.

She pulled out a large, rather heavy quilt. Spreading it on the floor, she saw the image of a scene she knew well. It was a green pasture surrounded by near and far-away mountains. White clouds floated in a pale blue sky. In the center of the pasture was a green mound with a little gazebo on top. Three cows were standing in front of the mound. A silver-gray river flowed beside the pasture toward the mountains, and brown rocks in the river had small, gold embroidered flowers on them.

It was the Nacoochee Valley and Chattahoochee River. The flowered rocks represented the meaning Katherine and her mother gave the word *Chattahoochee*. They thought the reason the Indians named the river "Marked Rocks" was because they had found rocks containing flecks of gold.

The quilt was made from hundreds of pieces of cloth, different shades of green, blue, and purple. Gray, silver, white, and brown also were hand-stitched together and combined with embroidery. The mound and cows' bodies had been slightly stuffed to rise from the surface of the quilt, and two-hole buttons gave the cows' heads a quirky charm. Katherine picked up the quilt and pressed it to her face, silently thanking her mother for such a precious gift.

"That is beautiful. Now can we eat?" Mrs. Martin said.

The three of them were seated at the table before Mr. Hill began explaining his reason for being in Atlanta.

"I am representing twenty-eight people in Helen who asked me to talk to Governor Talmadge. We want him to cooperate with President Roosevelt. I didn't get to come here as soon as I promised, and Talmadge is using the governor's office in the Capitol even though he hasn't yet been sworn in. I had to wait days before I actually talked to him."

Both Katherine and Mrs. Martin looked at him expectantly without speaking.

"He says he's not going to let the president put any of his CCC boys in Georgia. That means they won't be making any roads or dams in our mountains. Needless to say, it means they won't be planting any trees."

Katherine and Mrs. Martin knew that CCC referred to the Civilian Conservation Corps, the young men between the ages of seventeen and twenty-eight who would work on these projects with most of their pay sent home to their families.

Both women responded simultaneously, "Why?"

"I wrote myself a note of some of Talmadge's words," he said, pulling a piece of paper from his shirt pocket. "Please forgive me, but I want to use his exact words. He said, 'The New Deal is a combination of wet-nursing, frenzied finance, downright communism, and plain damned foolishness.' He said other similar words, but I know what his real objection is. The president is enrolling both white boys and colored boys in the CCC. It will help colored people as much as white people, and that's the reason Talmadge doesn't approve."

Mrs. Martin said, "What can we do?"

"You can write letters to Governor Talmadge. I'm going to write him a letter, and I'll ask others to do it. Maybe if he gets enough written requests, he'll change his mind."

Katherine wanted to see Callahan. She wanted to show him her new quilt, and she wanted to ask him about writing a letter to Talmadge. She suddenly realized that she was beginning to depend on him, and she didn't like it. She didn't realize that spending time with him was when she was most alive.

CHAPTER 14

TO WASHINGTON

Katherine and Mrs. Martin wrote separate letters to Talmadge, although Katherine didn't see Callahan to get his advice. It was almost two months before she saw him again.

Late in February, he was standing on the sidewalk as she exited Rich's. She saw him before he saw her, and she braced herself, wanting to greet him seriously and calmly, but she couldn't keep a large smile from her face.

"I've come to invite you and Mrs. Martin to go to Washington for President Roosevelt's inauguration," he said.

She didn't answer immediately. Washington was a long distance north of Atlanta, 650 miles.

"What do you mean?"

"We are arranging a special train to go from Warm Springs, and I know how you both wanted him to win the presidency. You both can get on the train when it stops here in Atlanta. I'll get you some tickets. You'll board in the evening and travel all night, but you won't be in a sleeper car. You'll have to sleep in your seats."

After hearing this, Katherine couldn't think of anything else. That evening she wrote her parents to tell them that she and Mrs. Martin would be going to Washington in March for the inauguration.

Their train tickets came to her later in an envelope marked "Personal" and delivered to Rich's.

Mrs. Martin and Katherine dressed in their best church clothes to catch the train. Katherine's dress was a stylish handmade favorite of black and beige. The beige was exactly the color of her hair. She wore her comfortable black shoes, polished to a vivid shine; black gloves; and a small black hat. A sweater provided all the extra warmth she needed while waiting for the train, and she carried a heavy black jacket with gloves in the pocket and a beige wool scarf for the weather in Washington.

Both women chose outfits that they thought would look good the next day after wearing them overnight. She knew some travelers purchased complete new outfits for the trip.

Governor Talmadge had a separate train going to Washington for most of Georgia's elected officials, their staffs, and families. New uniforms were purchased for all of Talmadge's officials, olive drab for day and white silk gabardine for evening with appropriate ornaments.

Crowds of well-wishers were at the terminal station, and a band played patriotic airs as the new passengers boarded the trains. Scout troops, high school choruses, and other school groups were among the passengers boarding the Warm Springs Special. News articles reported that the train had been arranged by two residents of Greenville, Georgia, and the Southern Railroad. It had a banner along the side that said "Warm Springs, Meriwether County, Roosevelt Special."

Residents of Meriwether County, who made friends with Roosevelt during his first visit to Warm Springs, were on board, still practicing the rural simplicity that they knew best. But it also contained people from all over the state. Sleeper cars called Pullman Palaces were filled with the Warm Springs rehabilitation center's physically disabled patients who represented fifteen states.

All together, the travelers on the Warm Springs Special totaled one thousand.

The Warm Springs train was the last to load in Atlanta and traveled two miles behind Governor Talmadge's deluxe train, which also carried one thousand travelers. The Talmadge train moved northward behind the Crescent Limited, which had more than five hundred Georgians going to the inauguration of their adopted son. Callahan was with other Roosevelt staffers on the Crescent.

When they were seated, Katherine looked around at the other passengers. Two couples ushering teenage children sat near them as well as a beautiful young woman who appeared to be traveling alone.

Katherine was sitting near the window, and as the train moved north, she saw people along the track who were viewing all three trains. They were waving and cheering, and some were saluting. She wondered how she could meet the young woman passenger because they might have a lot in common.

Shortly after they began traveling, Mrs. Martin said she was going to walk through the train and check out the other cars. When she left her seat, the young woman appeared and asked if she could join Katherine.

"I'm going to Roosevelt's inauguration and assume you are too. Have you been to Washington before?" she said.

Neither woman had been to Washington, and as they talked, Katherine learned her name was Mary Margaret Jones. Chris Callahan had invited her to the inauguration too.

Katherine didn't realize she had felt like his only special friend until she learned he also invited this young woman to make the trip.

"Did you work on the Roosevelt campaign?" Mary Margaret Jones said.

"No, I work at Rich's," Katherine said.

"My brother used to work there. His name is Elliot Jones. Do you know him?"

"Yes, he was in charge of women's wear, and that's where I work."

As their conversation continued, Mary Margaret eventually told Katherine that she and her brother didn't agree on politics. She said he wanted her to leave the Atlanta office of the Roosevelt campaign, but she refused. "He's a strong supporter of Governor Talmadge, but I'm not. Elliot is against Roosevelt, but I've been a supporter since he announced his plans." She leaned closer to Katherine. "My brother doesn't want colored people to gain anything. I don't know why he feels that way because that's not the way we were raised. He gets angry when I try to talk to him about it."

Their conversation was going strong when Mrs. Martin returned. Katherine left her seat and joined Mary Margaret near the front of the car.

"I wish Chris could be with us in this car," Mary Margaret said. Katherine wondered if Chris was committed to her. The more she tried to brush the idea from her mind, the more worried she felt. *He's only my friend. We've done nothing but talk about politics. I have no reason to feel this way.*

They were wondering what Washington would be like when Katherine went back to her seat to eat the sandwiches she and Mrs. Martin brought with them.

Mrs. Martin was excited to tell her that their friend, Will Jackson, was a porter on the Warm Springs train. "He showed me the entrance to the patients' cars, but we didn't go in. I don't know any of the patients, and I would only be gawking at them."

Roosevelt was the only Warm Springs patient who was often seen in public. Other patients suffering from paralysis were rarely seen, but stories about the patients were popular in the newspapers.

Katherine and Mrs. Martin had read about children who improved at Warm Springs. They also read about one nurse who lived in a machine called an iron lung, and she learned to stand alone in the water.

When the night's darkness prevented Katherine from seeing anything out the window, she closed her eyes and tried to close her mind. She wanted to get a good night's sleep, and the train was supposed to be in Washington about seven in the morning.

What was Chris Callahan to Elliot's sister? Was he committed to her? I've got to stop depending on him so much. I must remember that he is only a friend.

She was surprised that she had finally slept when she opened her eyes and saw beautifully landscaped scenery plus a pale gray monument of some kind in the distance. Later, her view was blocked

NEW BEGINNINGS

because the Warm Springs Special pulled in between two passenger trains at the Washington, DC, railroad terminal.

Katherine and Mrs. Martin departed their car and walked carefully between the trains into the huge Union Station. Each purchased a doughnut in the vast depot before following handwritten signs to a line of buses that were going to the Capitol for the inauguration. The day was gray and cold, not "Roosevelt weather."

The news media had begun talking about Roosevelt weather during the campaign when each day at a rally was warm and inviting.

On arrival they could see the festooned Capitol in the distance. They were among thousands of excited people, mostly men, and moved to what they hoped was a good place to see and hear the new president's inaugural address.

Official activities began at a quarter after ten with a short prayer. A long parade came down the street where they were standing and included a number of marching bands. A large group of palomino horses amazed Katherine. "I wonder where they found so many palominos that are so perfectly matched."

An open touring car with Franklin and Eleanor Roosevelt traveled by slowly to shouts of excitement. Later, they heard an announcement that Roosevelt's car was at the White House where Eleanor Roosevelt was giving her seat to outgoing President Herbert Hoover.

During the campaign, the two men had each promoted their dislike of the other, and now they had to sit side by side in the parade car. Roosevelt had won the majority of votes in forty-two of the forty-eight states, leaving only six states voting for Hoover.

Katherine and Mrs. Martin watched the car drive by slowly as Roosevelt waved his hat to the cheering crowd. The heavily defeated Hoover sat immobile.

After he was sworn in, Roosevelt stepped to the podium. He began, "This is preeminently the time to speak the truth, the whole truth, frankly and boldly." He listed problems of the Depression and said, "Only a foolish optimist can deny the dark realities of the moment."

Later, he continued, "Our greatest primary task is to put people to work." He made it clear that he felt it was the responsibility of the government to help people who were in dire straits through no fault of their own. The country's economic controls needed to be adjusted.

"Our great nation will endure as it has endured, will revive and prosper," the new president said.

Katherine thought she could see Callahan on the distant stage in the large group with Roosevelt, but she wasn't sure. After Roosevelt finished his address, she saw Callahan moving toward her and Mrs. Martin. He was talking and laughing with Mary Margaret Jones.

She moved quickly away after asking Mrs. Martin to go with her. They found a restaurant where they had to wait in line for service, and Mrs. Martin said she couldn't walk anymore. Katherine spent as much time in the restaurant as possible to let Mrs. Martin rest. She also thought that staying there would help her avoid seeing Callahan. She didn't want to see him with Mary Margaret Jones. At the same time, her mind was filled with the image of his handsome, smiling face and twinkling eyes.

She didn't want to talk to Callahan the way she had before. She didn't want to talk to Callahan at all. On the southbound train that evening, she didn't see Mary Margaret Jones and vowed that she must forget Chris Callahan.

CHAPTER 15

TREE ARMY

Back in Atlanta, Katherine began looking for a civic or political organization she might join. She knew she had to devote herself to a worthwhile cause so her happiness wouldn't depend on another person. She was not eligible for United Daughters of the Confederacy because she didn't have a relative who had served in the war.

Although she didn't want to think about Chris Callahan, she knew she must thank him for the trip to Washington for FDR's inauguration, but she didn't know how to contact him. He had frequently waited for her outside Rich's door and now he was never there. She had no idea if he had an office or a residence in Atlanta. After the inauguration, maybe he had stayed in Washington to help FDR's administration keep its campaign promises. Maybe he was helping with the New Deal.

Not knowing anything else to do, she wrote a thank-you note and signed it, "Wishing God's best for you, Katherine." She put Callahan's name first and then wrote "In care of FDR." On the next line, she wrote "Washington, DC." She had heard of poorly addressed letters reaching their destination, and maybe someone would pass this letter on to Callahan.

Now she had to join the church she had been attending and find a way to make a positive contribution to society. Rich's was one of the few businesses on Peachtree Street that had not closed, so she still had a salaried job.

The Chamber of Commerce had launched a program of sending starving families to abandoned farms around the city, but few families signed up because they had just come from the farms. Chamber organizers became afraid of creating riots. The City of Atlanta operated a relief center at its auditorium annex, which was jointly funded by Fulton County. A newspaper article said the city's relief center had served five hundred thousand meals the previous year and housed twenty thousand.

The church immediately offered Katherine a way to contribute. It did not operate its own soup kitchen, but its members helped at another church's kitchen. Katherine offered to help on the evenings she didn't have to work.

She became very worried after her first evening working at the church's kitchen because she learned that it served only white people with nothing for the dark complected. Talking to another volunteer, she was told, "Colored men can get thirty days free board and meals by going to jail and working in the chain gang."

She was trying to find a place that served all hungry citizens of Atlanta when she heard it described as "a transient city." Officials of both government and charitable organizations wanted to help only local citizens, but high numbers of families were passing through Atlanta as they attempted to find a supportive home.

One evening after she returned to her room, Mrs. Martin met her. "You have a letter from your friend," she said. She didn't say which friend but seemed excited.

Katherine stepped over to the little table where all the mail was placed. She stared and couldn't pick up the envelope. It was from Chris Callahan.

"Well, pick it up and read it," Mrs. Martin said, laughing. "It isn't going to bite you."

"I'll go to my room," Katherine said.

She carefully opened the envelope and slowly began reading.

NEW BEGINNINGS

Dear Katherine,

It is a miracle that I have your note thanking me for your trip to Washington. I have a good friend in the White House mailroom, and he saw it and gave it to me. I can't believe he saw it because our president has about five hundred letters coming in each day. I am so glad to have your return address.

You owe me nothing for the trip. I just wish I could have found you while you were here. I made a bad mistake when I didn't tell you where to wait for me. Of course I couldn't have shown you much in that short time.

I have to stay in Washington for an unknown length of time. The president has so much he wants to do quickly, and I want to help as much as I can. I've been typing letters and typing proposed laws to go before Congress.

The first thing the president had to do was stop people from losing their life's savings in banks. He wants to pay farmers for not planting part of their property so prices will rise and give them reason to grow crops again. Surplus crops have caused farm prices to drop out of site while, at the same time, people are dying for lack of food. We've heard of farmers burning their corn for fuel because the price is so low, and you don't want to hear about what some are doing with excess animals. He wants to create power-producing facilities owned by their consumers. This would provide electricity in the mountains and valleys and would eventually reach into Helen. There's more, but that's enough for now. The law drafts I type go before a group of lawyers who sometimes rewrite the whole proposal. I don't care what they change as long as Congress will pass them.

Please write to me and tell me what you are doing. I wish we could visit, but because that's impossible, let's keep in touch with letters.

I'll be waiting for your letters. My complete address is Chris Callahan, Hardman House, Room 302, Washington, DC.

Chris

Katherine couldn't go to bed without responding to Chris. She wrote a long letter and told him about her efforts to give something back to the community.

Time seemed to fly as she waited for his letters. Then a letter from her mother excited her and gave her something important to write about to Chris.

Dear Chris,

I received a letter from my mother today with this as the first sentence: Hank has a job.

Hank is married to my sister, and he's been without a steady job for more than two years. He, my sister Angel, and their baby boy had to move in with my parents.

A temporary CCC office opened in Cleveland, and he wanted to be first in the line of job applicants. He got there about five in the morning, and more than a dozen men were already waiting. Some had spent the night in line.

Now he's working with what everyone refers to as the tree army. He's in a camp on Smith Creek above Robertstown. He walks there to report early on Monday morning and walks back Friday evening. The camp has almost one hundred planters. They live in tents, and he said they have wonderful meals.

Our country's military army operates the camp, and the head cook at his camp is also with the US Army.

He couldn't tell Mom how many trees they have planted, but he said he takes a bucket of trees and a shovel and begins planting. When the bucket is empty, he goes back for more. Most of the other tree planters are from places in Georgia. He hasn't met any yet from another state.

He said a truck goes almost daily from the camp to Cleveland where it meets a truck from Gainesville. It comes back loaded with loaves of bread. They pass some houses where children are standing by the road, and they always throw out a loaf to them. The children fight, grab hunks of the bread, and have it completely eaten before the truck is gone. They are always there and seem to be waiting.

My mother can't believe trees are actually being planted. She's excited that someday the mountains may again be covered in beautiful trees.

We can't say enough thank-yous to God for giving us President Roosevelt. Not only is the president restoring the mountains, but he's also restoring my brother-in-law's faith in himself. That makes my family happy.

Hank told Mother that he might be moved to another camp called Vogel. The tree army will make a lake there and build cabins for campers. She thinks he wants to stop planting trees and begin building things. If he moves there, he won't be able to walk home for the weekend, but he can write letters home.

I still am looking for a way to help all citizens, regardless of their background.

> Thank you for your letters explaining your work.
> I never cease to be surprised at what you are doing.
> I'm always waiting for your letters.
>
> > Wishing you blessings,
> > Katherine

Katherine kept working at the soup kitchen, always saddened by families with small children. She regretted the derogatory comments she heard about its existence. One official said they were "making Atlanta into a beggars' paradise."

The City of Atlanta had created a new relief program that required application to the city warden for assistance. The warden was supposed to make sure the applicants were "worthy" and began investigations to confirm this.

Applications for relief were averaging twelve thousand a month, and if approved, a family received $10.12 a month. Unemployment reached 33 percent, but in the black neighborhoods, unemployment was 75 percent. The warden's investigations into worthiness swamped the city's system.

Concerns about hungry black children caused Katherine to visit her new black friend, Dinah Sue Jackson. After talking a bit with Dinah Sue, Katherine asked, "What can I do to help colored people?"

"I know you want to help," Dinah Sue said, "but there's nothing you can do. The culture doesn't allow you to help. You know that white people would be upset if you attempted to start assistance for colored people."

Katherine didn't respond, and after a minute, Dinah Sue said, "Colored people have to learn to help themselves. We have to find a way to work through the thick maze and become self-sufficient. Maybe you don't know, but when colored babies are born, they think they are like all other people. Then, when they learn to walk and talk, they are told they are sons and daughters of slaves. Anytime they try something different, other colored people object and tell them again that they are children of slaves. Colored children are mentally defeated by the time they are ten years old."

Again Katherine didn't respond. Finally she said, "It's all so unfair."

"Maybe you can do something to change the mind-set of white people. I guess white children are told the same thing about colored children. That sets their thinking. All children are born into a web that entangles them from the start. I think it will be gone someday, but it will take a long, long time," Dinah Sue said.

Katherine said she didn't mind expressing her opinion but admitted she was afraid of members of the KKK. "I'll keep trying to make a difference," she said. Then they talked about Dinah Sue's upcoming wedding, and Katherine wished her well.

CHAPTER 16

HOME AGAIN

Katherine was planning to buy her own car and learn to drive when the month of June arrived and put Georgia in the most beautiful part of summer. She wished she could visit with Dinah Sue Jackson every day, but their paths didn't cross, and she couldn't go to her house unless Mrs. Martin drove her.

She began noticing the words of Eleanor Roosevelt, the country's first lady. The first comment she read and quoted frequently in her mind was "Do what you feel in your heart to be right. You'll be criticized anyway."

All her plans changed when she received a letter from Chris saying that he would be visiting Atlanta. She immediately made plans to meet his train the following Friday afternoon, and she put her favorite dress to the side with plans to wear it to work that day. She wanted to look her best for him.

She thought about the upcoming meeting all day Thursday at work. She didn't know what she would say or what would happen, but she wanted him to know how happy she was that he was back.

Leaving work Thursday evening, she saw a figure outside on the sidewalk that looked strangely familiar. As she opened the glass door to step outside, she found herself in the arms of Chris Callahan.

After laughing up into his face, she found her lips sealed in a long kiss.

Wrapped in a cocoon of happiness, she hugged him again.

NEW BEGINNINGS

"How could you arrive today? I was looking for you tomorrow evening."

"I came by air."

"Did you fly in on a Delta crop duster?"

Chris laughed. "No, I came by American Airways. Congress is investigating the awarding of air-mail contracts, and I'm learning as much as I can about the different airlines."

"Well, I asked permission to have Saturday off from work so I could spend time with you, but I have to work tomorrow."

"That's great because I want to drive you to Helen on Saturday."

Friday was a blur for Katherine. She tried to be efficient and attentive to customers, but her mind was filled with thoughts of Chris Callahan. Callahan was busy planning their automobile trip of almost one hundred miles on Georgia roads. Katherine was surprised at the idea because she had made the trip only by train.

Chris telephoned the sheriffs of Gwinnett County, Hall County, and White County to ask them about the local condition of the road to Helen. He assumed the road in north Fulton County would be passable. After learning that the roads were "okay, not too choppy," he estimated the time of their trip and called Helen with a message for Katherine's father, giving him an estimation of their arrival time in Helen "if there was no accident or engine failure."

He drove her to Mrs. Martin's Friday evening where an elaborate supper was prepared for them. Mrs. Martin appeared to be as pleased as Katherine with his arrival.

When he left, Chris kissed Katherine again and said, "I'll pick you up at seven tomorrow morning." Katherine wished she had time to write to her parents and tell them they were coming. She didn't know Chris had already told them.

They began their trip at seven o'clock as planned. Parts of the road had old paving, sometimes badly broken, and large sections of the road were not paved. Chris was driving slowly and carefully to avoid the biggest bumps, but he didn't let his concentration on the road keep him from talking about an important automobile caravan on the same road more than ten years earlier.

"I know you've been worried that Helen and the mountains would lose their beauty and be gone," he said. "I want our trip today to honor a forest expedition made more than ten years ago in an effort to make people aware of how valuable the mountains are. It was organized by the *Atlanta Constitution* to promote the idea of making the northeast Georgia mountains and your old home into a protected forest and national playground. Mary Margaret Jones found several newspaper articles about the expedition and thought you'd like them" He didn't give Katherine time to ask about Mary Margaret as he continued talking.

"Forty government officials made the trip and filled twelve cars. At every town, others joined them, and the caravan's final total was fifty cars. Some of them spent the night in Helen," he said.

"I'm sure Mom and Dad will remember their visit," Katherine said.

"The news articles about this said there wasn't a more beautiful region anywhere. The expedition promoted a national forest plus better roads. Easier travel will come and bring visitors in droves. That means your town is going to live again. Not only Helen but also Dahlonega, Blairsville, Clayton, all the towns. The trees will grow, and visitors will come. Just imagine that your mountains will again be a beautiful reason to celebrate," Chris said. He was too committed to the expedition's purpose to slow his words.

"The president is looking at the possibility of running lines of electricity into all the rural areas, as well as good roads into the forests. And I hope we can live long enough to see the results," he said.

Katherine could not imagine a constant flow of visitors to Helen and the mountains. She had no idea what such a situation would be like. The idea was too strange for her to be able to make smart comments.

Almost three hours after they began, their car entered Gainesville. "That forest expedition was gigantic when it reached this town that calls itself the 'Gateway to the Mountains.' Flags were flying here, and beautiful girls were throwing flowers at the officials."

NEW BEGINNINGS

As Chris said these words, he turned their car down a smooth street toward Brenau College. Four lovely girls ran toward the road. He stopped the car, got out, and invited Katherine to join him as the girls watched. She stood by the car, uncertain of his purpose, when he dropped to his knee in front of her. "Will you marry me?" he asked.

After hesitating, Katherine said, "Of course."

Caught in his hug, she saw flowers being thrown at them by the laughing, cheering girls.

Chris introduced the girls and said one was the daughter of his friend, a Georgia legislator. "She and her friends caught the Warm Springs train to Washington for the inauguration. This is another big day for me, and they wanted to be a part of it," he said.

Back in the car, Katherine looked at her diamond engagement ring. "My parents will be so surprised. They'll be glad to meet you, and I wish they already knew you."

"It's easy to get your father to a Helen telephone. I talked to him last week and asked him for your hand. I talked to him again on the telephone yesterday," Chris said. "After our wedding, I want you to live with me in Washington."

Katherine was surprised and remained silent for several miles. "I want to find something where I can continue to give something back. I believe in Jesus, and my church helps me meet the challenges of life. I hope you will go to church with me," she said.

"Sure. I know you always go to church, and I too want to give something back. I've been attending a church in Washington. I think you'll like it."

"Participating in activities at a church helps us learn more about Jesus's teachings. It helps us choose the right path when life becomes a challenge," said Katherine, repeating words from her father.

"Don't forget that it should give us a better understanding of people who we initially want to snub, even other members of church. I always remind myself that Jesus loved all people," Callahan said.

"I can see I'm not telling you anything you don't already know. When we get to Helen, you must tell Daddy that we will join a church in Washington."

She and Chris were lost in their own thoughts as they traveled the last miles to Helen. Bouncing across the little covered bridge and gaining a view of Helen, they saw two young boys running beside the car. It was Katherine's brothers, John and Joe. As Katherine saw the stone arch entrance to the hotel, she saw her mother, her father, and Angel get up from a roadside bench. Angel was holding Hank Jr., and Katherine's mother was holding a bouquet of mountain laurel. Each person was grinning ear to ear.

Hugs and exclamations of love filled the air before Chris parked the car and they all walked up to the old hotel restaurant. Seated around a table and waiting for their food, Katherine's mother said, "I wish Hank could be with us, but he's at Vogel. He's so proud of what they're creating there. He works diligently from dawn to dusk, and he loves it."

Chris responded to her. "Maam, our president wants these mountains to be a forest wonderland again."

Katherine's mother said, "He's not the only one. We traveled to Tray Mountain a couple of years ago, and all the stumpland and red ditches left me very depressed. We didn't even see birds. We've been praying that the mountains could be restored."

AFTERWORD

I was almost 80 years old when I wrote this book, and grew up near Helen, so much of it is from my actual memory. Some of it is based on the stories my mother told me, and much of it is based on actual characters I knew. Study and intense, specific research for this book began about 2006. I wanted to tell actual facts about the giant Helen sawmill, the disappearance of the mountains' trees, and the reforestation by the Civilian Conservation Corps during the Franklin Delano Roosevelt administration.

The many people who knowingly or unknowingly gave me information for this book cannot all be named, but one stands out in my mind. That is the late Dr. Tom Lumsden, a medical doctor in the Nacoochee Valley and longtime collector of local history. He told me about going into the sawmill as a child and shared his entire historical file on the town of Helen. I visited Mildred W. Greear of Helen and talked to her and her husband. I visited people in nursing homes and asked them to share memories of growing up in or near Helen. I visited David Greear, who patiently helped me find photos from old Helen.

I am grateful to friends who read the manuscript and especially grateful to Carolyn who helped me start writing again after I hit what I thought was insurmountable blockage.

I read the beginning of the book *Matthews: The Historic Adventures of a Pioneer Family*, which began with the family's purchase of northeast Georgia property for a sawmill and establishment of the railroad. This gave me details I needed for more research, and I found written personal experiences from a large sawmill in North Carolina.

I also read all the information available in the White County History Museum and read the rare written history of one local church.

I read numerous books about the era, including *The Wild Man from Sugar Creek*, which tells of Georgia's sixty-seventh governor, Eugene Talmadge. I was glad to visit the new Civilian Conservation Corps Museum at Vogel State Park. There, a museum representative told me that the CCC planted twenty-three million trees in Georgia and erected four thousand miles of phone lines.

I did major research in the *Atlanta Journal* and *Atlanta Constitution* archives, reading many articles about Helen, the Nacoochee Valley, and the mountains. The giant motorcade of elected officials that promoted protection of the mountains left Atlanta on May 29, 1922. More cars joined the motorcade in each town, and beautiful girls threw flowers at the cars as it passed through Gainesville.

Only one character mentioned in this book is real. That is Arthur Woody, also known as "Kingfish" or "The Barefoot Ranger." Woody was born and lived in Suches, Georgia, about thirty miles north of Helen. He and Ranger Nick Nicholson are considered the most important figures in the creation of the Chattahoochee National Forest. All other characters in this book are fictitious, but their comments, ideas, and actions come from the many people I knew or interviewed with this book in mind. They also come from stories I heard about Georgia mountain people and my mother's stories about life.

The black woman who continued to get her monthly pay from a white family after becoming bedridden is based on a real person.

All historical facts, including the Crescent and two special trains of supporters going from Georgia to Washington, DC, for President Roosevelt's inauguration, are real.

EPILOGUE

In 1936, the Chattahoochee National Forest was born. In 2016, at the writing of this book, the forest covered great portions of eighteen North Georgia counties, including White County. The forest has 450 miles of hiking trails, more than 1,600 miles of easy travel roads, and 2,200 miles of rivers and streams. Ten sections have been designated "Wilderness Areas," which means that the trees cannot be harvested.

The Chattahoochee National Forest also includes the beginning of the 2,174-mile Appalachian Trail at Springer Mountain in Georgia, as well as Georgia's highest point, Brasstown Bald, which is 4,784 feet high.

The beauty of the forest and its easy access now are causing problems. Urban sprawl is encroaching on the forest's southern border. Roads to benefit loggers have provided frequent sightseers with access to sensitive areas. Other sightseers have abused trails designated for their use.

The southern pine beetle has destroyed acres of trees, the habitat for flora, fauna, and forest animals. The woolly adelgid is a threat to the stately hemlock, a popular ornamental tree sometimes used in landscapes.

National Forest Service personnel work diligently in management of the forest.

Georgia had 127 Civilian Conservation Corps camps, with thirty to thirty-five Georgia camps operating at a time. Visitors to Vogel State Park and Lake Winfield Scott State Park in northeast Georgia still enjoy the cabins and lakes built by the CCC.

President Franklin Roosevelt was elected three more times and died suddenly at the Little White House in Warm Springs in 1945.

In Helen in 1968, owners of the town's old buildings became concerned when cars traveled through without stopping. They used their own money to change the town into a Bavarian Alpine village. Major newspapers in the United States and Europe reported the townspeople's ingenuity and published photos of the remodeled buildings. Thus, Alpine Helen became a major tourist attraction.

The old granary, called Nora Mill, is unchanged and still grinds corn and wheat products. The Italianate house that Bennie thought resembled a fairy tale mansion has been restored and is now the Hardman Farm Historic Site, operated by the nearby Smithgall Woods State Park. The Indian mound still has the same beautiful gazebo on top, and passersby still think of the Cherokee Indian braves who ran down the mound and into the Chattahoochee River to cool off after a vibrant ceremony.

www.ingramcontent.com/pod-product-compliance
Ingram Content Group UK Ltd.
Pitfield, Milton Keynes, MK11 3LW, UK
UKHW022227230426
12048UKWH00016BA/1118